A CHANCE ACQUAINTANCE

W. D. HOWELLS

1st WORLD
LIBRARY
Literary Society

A Chance Acquaintance

W. D. Howells

© 1st World Library, 2006
PO Box 2211
Fairfield, IA 52556
www.1stworldlibrary.com
First Edition

LCCN: 2007920708

Softcover ISBN: 978-1-4218-4016-1
Hardcover ISBN: 978-1-4218-3916-5
eBook ISBN: 978-1-4218-4116-8

Purchase *"A Chance Acquaintance"*
as a traditional bound book at:
www.1stWorldLibrary.com/purchase.asp?ISBN=978-1-4218-4016-1

1st World Library is a literary, educational organization
dedicated to:

- Creating a free internet library of downloadable ebooks

- Hosting writing competitions and offering book
  publishing scholarships.

1ˢᵗ World Library Literary Society

Giving Back to the World

"If you want to work on the core problem, it's early school literacy."

- James Barksdale, former CEO of Netscape

"No skill is more crucial to the future of a child, or to a democratic and prosperous society, than literacy."

- Los Angeles Times

Literacy... means far more than learning how to read and write... The aim is to transmit... knowledge and promote social participation."

- UNESCO

"Literacy is not a luxury, it is a right and a responsibility. If our world is to meet the challenges of the twenty-first century we must harness the energy and creativity of all our citizens."

- President Bill Clinton

"Parents should be encouraged to read to their children, and teachers should be equipped with all available techniques for teaching literacy, so the varying needs and capacities of individual kids can be taken into account."

- Hugh Mackay

I

UP THE SAGUENAY

On the forward promenade of the Saguenay boat which had been advertised to leave Quebec at seven o'clock on Tuesday morning, Miss Kitty Ellison sat tranquilly expectant of the joys which its departure should bring, and tolerantly patient of its delay; for if all the Saguenay had not been in promise, she would have thought it the greatest happiness just to have that prospect of the St. Lawrence and Quebec. The sun shone with a warm yellow light on the Upper Town, with its girdle of gray wall, and on the red flag that drowsed above the citadel, and was a friendly lustre on the tinned roofs of the Lower Town; while away off to the south and east and west wandered the purple hills and the farmlit plains in such dewy shadow and effulgence as would have been enough to make the heaviest heart glad. Near at hand the river was busy with every kind of craft, and in the distance was mysterious with silvery vapors; little breaths of haze, like an ethereal colorless flame, exhaled from its surface, and it all glowed with a lovely inner radiance. In the middle distance a black ship was heaving anchor and setting sail, and the voice of the seamen came soft and sad and yet wildly hopeful to the dreamy ear of the young girl, whose soul at once went round the world before the ship, and then made haste back again to the promenade of the Saguenay boat. She sat leaning forward a little with her hands fallen into her lap, letting her unmastered thoughts play as they would in memories and hopes around the consciousness that she was the happiest girl in the world, and blest beyond desire or desert.

To have left home as she had done, equipped for a single day at Niagara, and then to have come adventurously on, by grace of her cousin's wardrobe, as it were, to Montreal and Quebec; to be now going up the Saguenay, and finally to be destined to return home by way of Boston and New York;—this was more than any one human being had a right to; and, as she had written home to the girls, she felt that her privileges ought to be divided up among all the people of Eriecreek. She was very grateful to Colonel Ellison and Fanny for affording her these advantages; but they being now out of sight in pursuit of state-rooms, she was not thinking of them in relation to her pleasure in the morning scene, but was rather regretting the absence of a lady with whom they had travelled from Niagara, and to whom she imagined she would that moment like to say something in praise of the prospect. This lady was a Mrs. Basil March of Boston; and though it was her wedding journey and her husband's presence ought to have absorbed her, she and Miss Kitty had sworn a sisterhood, and were pledged to see each other before long at Mrs. March's home in Boston. In her absence, now, Kitty thought what a very charming person she was, and wondered if all Boston people were really like her, so easy and friendly and hearty. In her letter she had told the girls to tell her Uncle Jack that he had not rated Boston people a bit too high, if she were to judge from Mr. and Mrs. March, and that she was sure they would help her as far as they could to carry out his instructions when she got to Boston.

These instructions were such as might seem preposterous if no more particular statement in regard to her Uncle Jack were made, but will be imaginable enough, I hope, when he is a little described. The Ellisons were a West Virginia family who had wandered up into a corner of Northwestern New York, because Dr. Ellison (unceremoniously known to Kitty as Uncle Jack) was too much an abolitionist to live in a slaveholding State with safety to himself or comfort to his neighbors. Here his family of three boys and two girls had grown up, and hither in time had come Kitty, the only child of his youngest brother, who had gone first to Illinois and thence, from the pretty constant adversity of a country editor, to Kansas, where he

W. D. Howells

joined the Free State party and fell in one of the border feuds. Her mother had died soon after, find Dr. Ellison's heart bowed itself tenderly over the orphan. She was something not only dear, but sacred to him as the child of a martyr to the highest cause on earth; and the love of the whole family encompassed her. One of the boys had brought her from Kansas when she was yet very little, and she had grown up among them as their youngest sister; but the doctor, from a tender scruple against seeming to usurp the place of his brother in her childish thought, would not let her call him father, and in obedience to the rule which she soon began to give their love, they all turned and called him Uncle Jack with her. Yet the Ellisons, though they loved their little cousin, did not spoil her,—neither the doctor, nor his great grown-up sons whom she knew as the boys, nor his daughters whom she called the girls, though they were wellnigh women when she came to them. She was her uncle's pet and most intimate friend, riding with him on his professional visits till she became as familiar a feature of his equipage as the doctor's horse itself; and he educated her in those extreme ideas, tempered by humor, which formed the character of himself and his family. They loved Kitty, and played with her, and laughed at her when she needed ridiculing; they made a jest of their father on the one subject on which he never jested, and even the antislavery cause had its droll points turned to the light. They had seen danger and trouble enough at different times in its service, but no enemy ever got more amusement out of it. Their house was a principal *entrepot* of the underground railroad, and they were always helping anxious travellers over the line; but the boys seldom came back from an excursion to Canada without adventures to keep the family laughing for a week; and they made it a serious business to study the comic points of their beneficiaries, who severally lived in the family records by some grotesque mental or physical trait. They had an irreverent name among themselves for each of the humorless abolition lecturers who unfailingly abode with them on their rounds; and these brethren and sisters, as they called them, paid with whatever was laughable in them for the substantial favors they received.

Miss Kitty, having the same natural bent, began even as a child to share in these harmless reprisals, and to look at life with the same wholesomely fantastic vision. But she remembered one abolition visitor of whom none of them made fun, but treated with a serious distinction and regard,—an old man with a high, narrow forehead, and thereon a thick upright growth of gray hair; who looked at her from under bushy brows with eyes as of blue flame, and took her on his knee one night and sang to her "Blow ye the trumpet, blow!" He and her uncle had been talking of some indefinite, far-off place that they called Boston, in terms that commended it to her childish apprehension as very little less holy than Jerusalem, and as the home of all the good and great people outside of Palestine.

In fact, Boston had always been Dr. Ellison's foible. In the beginning of the great antislavery agitation, he had exchanged letters (corresponded, he used to say) with John Quincy Adams on the subject of Lovejoy's murder; and he had met several Boston men at the Free Soil Convention in Buffalo in 1848. "A little formal perhaps, a little reserved," he would say, "but excellent men; polished, and certainly of sterling principle": which would make his boys and girls laugh, as they grew older, and sometimes provoke them to highly colored dramatizations of the formality of these Bostonians in meeting their father. The years passed and the boys went West, and when the war came, they took service in Iowa and Wisconsin regiments. By and by the President's Proclamation of freedom to the slaves reached Eriecreek while Dick and Bob happened both to be home on leave. After they had allowed their sire his rapture, "Well, this is a great blow for father," said Bob; "what are you going to do now, father? Fugitive slavery and all its charms blotted out forever, at one fell swoop. Pretty rough on you, isn't it? No more men and brothers, no more soulless oligarchy. Dull lookout, father."

"O no," insinuated one of the girls, "there's Boston."

"Why, yes," cried Dick, "to be sure there is. The President hasn't abolished Boston. Live for Boston."

And the doctor did live for an ideal Boston, thereafter, so far at least as concerned a never-relinquished, never-fulfilled purpose of some day making a journey to Boston. But in the mean time there were other things; and at present, since the Proclamation had given him a country worth living in, he was ready to honor her by studying her antiquities. In his youth, before his mind had been turned so strenuously to the consideration of slavery, he had a pretty taste for the mystery of the Mound Builders, and each of his boys now returned to camp with instructions to note any phenomena that would throw light upon this interesting subject. They would have abundant leisure for research, since the Proclamation, Dr. Ellison insisted, practically ended the war.

The Mound Builders were only a starting-point for the doctor. He advanced from them to historical times in due course, and it happened that when Colonel Ellison and his wife stopped off at Eriecreek on their way East, in 1870, they found him deep in the history of the Old French War. As yet the colonel had not intended to take the Canadian route eastward, and he escaped without the charges which he must otherwise have received to look up the points of interest at Montreal and Quebec connected with that ancient struggle. He and his wife carried Kitty with them to see Niagara (which she had never seen because it was so near); but no sooner had Dr. Ellison got the despatch announcing that they would take Kitty on with them down the St. Lawrence to Quebec, and bring her home by way of Boston, than he sat down and wrote her a letter of the most comprehensive character. As far as concerned Canada his mind was purely historical; but when it came to Boston it was strangely re-abolitionized, and amidst an ardor for the antiquities of the place, his old love for its humanitarian pre-eminence blazed up. He would have her visit Faneuil Hall because of its Revolutionary memories, but not less because Wendell Phillips had there made his first antislavery speech. She was to see the collections of the Massachusetts Historical Society, and if possible certain points of ancient colonial interest which he named; but at any rate she was somehow to catch sight of the author of the "Biglow Papers," of Senator

Sumner, of Mr. Whittier, of Dr. Howe, of Colonel Higginson, and of Mr. Garrison. These people were all Bostonians to the idealizing remoteness of Dr. Ellison, and he could not well conceive of them asunder. He perhaps imagined that Kitty was more likely to see them together than separately; and perhaps indeed they were less actual persons, to his admiration, than so many figures of a grand historical composition. Finally, "I want you to remember, my dear child," he wrote, "that in Boston you are not only in the birthplace of American liberty, but the yet holier scene of its resurrection. There everything that is noble and grand and liberal and enlightened in the national life has originated, and I cannot doubt that you will find the character of its people marked by every attribute of a magnanimous democracy. If I could envy you anything, my dear girl, I should envy you this privilege of seeing a city where man is valued simply and solely for what he is in himself, and where color, wealth, family, occupation, and other vulgar and meretricious distinctions are wholly lost sight of in the consideration of individual excellence."

Kitty got her uncle's letter the night before starting up the Saguenay, and quite too late for compliance with his directions concerning Quebec; but she resolved that as to Boston his wishes should be fulfilled to the utmost limit of possibility. She knew that nice Mr. March must be acquainted with some of those very people. Kitty had her uncle's letter in her pocket, and she was just going to take it out and read it again, when something else attracted her notice.

The boat had been advertised to leave at seven o'clock, and it was now half past. A party of English people were pacing somewhat impatiently up and down before Kitty, for it had been made known among the passengers (by that subtle process through which matters of public interest transpire in such places) that breakfast would not be served till the boat started, and these English people had the appetites which go before the admirable digestions of their nation. But they had also the good temper which does not so certainly accompany the insular good appetite. The man in his dashing Glengarry

W. D. Howells

cap and his somewhat shabby gray suit took on one arm the plain, jolly woman who seemed to be his wife, and on the other, the amiable, handsome young girl who looked enough like him to be his sister, and strode rapidly back and forth, saying that they must get up an appetite for breakfast. This made the women laugh, and so he said it again, which made them laugh so much that the elder lost her balance, and in regaining it twisted off her high shoe-heel, which she briskly tossed into the river. But she sat down after that, and the three were presently intent upon the Liverpool steamer which was just arrived and was now gliding up to her dock, with her population of passengers thronging her quarter-deck.

"She's from England!" said the husband, expressively.

"Only fancy!" answered the wife. "Give me the glass, Jenny." Then, after a long survey of the steamer, she added, "Fancy her being from England!" They all looked and said nothing for two or three minutes, when the wife's mind turned to the delay of their own boat and of breakfast. "This thing," she said, with that air of uttering a novelty which the English cast about their commonplaces,—"this this thing doesn't start at seven, you know."

"No," replied the younger woman, "she waits for the Montreal boat."

"Fancy her being from England!" said the other, whose eyes and thoughts had both wandered back to the Liverpool steamer.

"There's the Montreal boat now, comin' round the point," cried the husband. "Don't you see the steam?" He pointed with his glass, and then studied the white cloud in the distance. "No, by Jove! it's a saw-mill on the shore."

"O Harry!" sighed both the women, reproachfully.

"Why, deuce take it, you know," he retorted, "I didn't turn it into a saw-mill. It's been a saw-mill all along, I fancy."

Half an hour later, when the Montreal boat came in sight, the women would have her a saw-mill till she stood in full view in mid-channel. Their own vessel paddled out into the stream as she drew near, and the two bumped and rubbed together till a gangway plank could he passed from one to the other. A very well dressed young man stood ready to get upon the Saguenay boat, with a porter beside him bearing his substantial valise. No one else apparently was coming aboard.

The English people looked upon him for an instant with wrathful eyes, as they hung over the rail of the promenade. "Upon my word," said the elder of the women, "have we been waitin' all this time for one man?"

"Hush, Edith," answered the younger, "it's an Englishman." And they all three mutely recognized the right of the Englishman to stop, not only the boat, but the whole solar system, if his ticket entitled him to a passage on any particular planet, while Mr. Miles Arbuton of Boston, Massachusetts, passed at his ease from one vessel to the other. He had often been mistaken for an Englishman, and the error of those spectators, if he had known it, would not have surprised him. Perhaps it might have softened his judgment of them as he sat facing them at breakfast; but he did not know it, and he thought them three very common English people with something professional, as of public singing or acting, about them. The young girl wore, instead of a travelling-suit, a vivid light blue dress; and over her sky-blue eyes and fresh cheeks a glory of corn-colored hair lay in great braids and masses. It was magnificent, but it wanted distance; so near, it was almost harsh. Mr. Arbuton's eyes fell from the face to the vivid blue dress, which was not quite fresh and not quite new, and a glimmer of cold dismissal came into them, as he gave himself entirely to the slender merits of the steamboat breakfast.

He was himself, meantime, an object of interest to a young lady who sat next to the English party, and who glanced at him from time to time, out of tender gray eyes, with a furtive play of feeling upon a sensitive face. To her he was that divine possibility which every young man is to every young maiden; and, besides, he was invested with a halo of romance as the gentleman with the blond mustache, whom she had seen at Niagara the week before, on the Goat Island Bridge. To the pretty matron at her side, he was exceedingly handsome, as a young man may frankly be to a young matron, but not otherwise comparable to her husband, the full-personed good-humored looking gentleman who had just added sausage to the ham and eggs on his plate. He was handsome, too, but his full beard was reddish, whereas Mr. Arbuton's mustache was flaxen; and his dress was not worn with that scrupulosity with which the Bostonian bore his clothes; there was a touch of slovenliness in him that scarcely consorted with the alert, ex-military air of some of his movements. "Good-looking young John Bull," he thought concerning Mr. Arbuton, and then thought no more about him, being no more self-judged before the supposed Englishman than he would have been before so much Frenchman or Spaniard. Mr. Arbuton, on the other hand, if he had met an Englishman so well dressed as himself, must at once have arraigned himself, and had himself tacitly tried for his personal and national difference. He looked in his turn at these people, and thought he should have nothing to do with them, in spite of the long-lashed gray eyes.

It was not that they had made the faintest advance towards acquaintance, or that the choice of knowing them or not was with Mr. Arbuton; but he had the habit of thus protecting himself from the chances of life, and a conscience against encouraging people whom he might have to drop for reasons of society. This was sometimes a sacrifice, for he was not past the age when people take a lively interest in most other human beings. When breakfast was over, and he had made the tour of the boat, and seen all his fellow-passengers, he perceived that he could have little in common with any of them, and that probably the journey would require the full exercise of that tolerant spirit in which he had undertaken a branch of summer travel in his native land.

The rush of air against the steamer was very raw and chill, and the forward promenade was left almost entirely to the English professional people, who walked rapidly up and down, with jokes and laughter of their kind, while the wind blew the girl's hair in loose gold about her fresh face, and twisted her blue drapery tight about her comely shape. When they got out of breath they sat down beside a large American lady, with a great deal of gold filling in her front teeth, and presently rose again and ran races to and from the bow. Mr. Arbuton turned away in displeasure. At the stern he found a much larger company, most of whom had furnished themselves with novels and magazines from the stock on board and were drowsing over them. One gentleman was reading aloud to three ladies the newspaper account of a dreadful shipwreck; other ladies and gentlemen were coming and going forever from their state-rooms, as the wont of some is; others yet sat with closed eyes, as if having come to see the Saguenay they were resolved to see nothing of the St. Lawrence on the way thither, but would keep their vision sacred to the wonders of the former river.

Yet the St. Lawrence was worthy to be seen, as even Mr. Arbuton owned, whose way was to slight American scenery, in distinction from his countrymen who boast it the finest in the world. As you leave Quebec, with its mural-crowned and castled rock, and drop down the stately river, presently the snowy fall of Montmorenci, far back in its purple hollow, leaps perpetual avalanche into the abyss, and then you are abreast of the beautiful Isle of Orleans, whose low shores, with their expanses of farmland, and their groves of pine and oak, are still as lovely as when the wild grape festooned the primitive forests and won from the easy rapture of old Cartier the name of Isle of Bacchus. For two hours farther down the river either shore is bright and populous with the continuous villages of the *habitans*, each clustering about its slim-spired church, in its shallow vale by the water's edge, or lifted in more eminent picturesqueness upon some gentle height. The banks, nowhere lofty or abrupt, are such as in a southern land some majestic river might flow between, wide, slumbrous, open to all the heaven and the long day till the very set of sun. But no starry palm glasses its crest in the clear cold green from these low brinks; the pale birch, slender and delicately fair, mirrors here the wintry whiteness of its boughs; and this is the sad great river of the awful North.

Gradually, as the day wore on, the hills which had shrunk almost out of sight on one hand, and on the other were dark purple in the distance, drew near the shore, and at one point on the northern side rose almost from the water's edge. The river expanded into a lake before them, and in their lap some cottages, and half-way up the hillside, among the stunted pines, a much-galleried hotel, proclaimed a resort of fashion in the heart of what seemed otherwise a wilderness. Indian huts sheathed in birch-bark nestled at the foot of the rocks, which were rich in orange and scarlet stains; out of the tops of the huts curled the blue smoke, and at the door of one stood a squaw in a flame-red petticoat; others in bright shawls squatted about on the rocks, each with a circle of dogs and papooses. But all this warmth of color only served, like a winter sunset, to heighten the chilly and desolate sentiment of the scene. The light dresses of the ladies on the veranda struck cold upon the eye; in the faces of the sojourners who lounged idly to the steamer's landing-place, the passenger could fancy a sad resolution to repress their tears when the boat should go away and leave them. She put off two or three old peasant-women who were greeted by other such on the pier, as if returned from a long journey; and then the crew discharged the vessel of a prodigious freight of onions which formed the sole luggage these old women had brought from Quebec. Bale after bale of the pungent bulbs were borne ashore in the careful arms of the deck-hands, and counted by the owners; at last order was given to draw in the plank, when a passionate cry burst from one of the old women, who extended both hands with an imploring gesture towards the boat. A bale of onions had been left aboard; a deck-hand seized it and ran quickly ashore with it, and then back again, followed by the benedictions of the tranquillized and comforted beldam. The gay sojourners at Murray Bay controlled their grief, and as Mr. Arbuton turned from them, the boat, pushing out, left them to their fashionable desolation. She struck across to the southern shore, to land passengers for Cacouna, a watering-place greater than Murray Bay. The tide, which rises fifteen feet at Quebec, is the impulse, not the savor of the sea; but at Cacouna the water is salt, and the sea-bathing lacks nothing but the surf; and hither resort in great numbers the Canadians who fly their cities during the fierce, brief fever of the northern summer. The watering-place village and hotel is not in sight from the landing, but, as at Murray Bay, the sojourners thronged the pier, as if the arrival of the steamboat were the great event of their day. That afternoon they were in unusual force, having come on foot and by omnibus and calash; and presently there passed down through their ranks a strange procession with a band of music leading the way to the steamer.

"It's an Indian wedding," Mr. Arbuton heard one of the boat's officers saying to the gentleman with the ex-military air, who stood next him beside the rail; and now, the band having drawn aside, he saw the bride and groom,—the latter a common, stolid-faced savage, and the former pretty and almost white, with a certain modesty and sweetness of mien. Before them went a young American, with a jaunty Scotch cap and a visage of supernatural gravity, as the master of ceremonies which he had probably planned; arm in arm with him walked a portly chieftain in black broadcloth, preposterously adorned on the breast with broad flat disks of silver in two rows. Behind the bridal couple came the whole village in pairs, men and women, and children of all ages, even to brown babies in arms, gay in dress and indescribably serious in demeanor. They were mated in some sort according to years and size; and the last couple were young fellows paired in an equal tipsiness. These reeled and wavered along the pier; and when the other wedding guests crowned the day's festivity by going aboard the steamer, they followed dizzily down the gangway. Midway they lurched heavily; the spectators gave a cry; but they had happily lurched in opposite directions; their grip upon each other's arms held, and a forward stagger launched them victoriously aboard in a heap. They had scarcely disappeared from sight, when, having as it were instantly satisfied their

W. D. Howells

curiosity concerning the boat, the other guests began to go ashore in due order. Mr. Arbuton waited in a slight anxiety to see whether the tipsy couple could repeat their maneuver successfully on an upward incline; and they had just appeared on the gangway, when he felt a hand passed carelessly and as if unconsciously through his arm, and at the same moment a voice said, "Those are a pair of disappointed lovers, I suppose."

He looked round and perceived the young lady of the party he had made up his mind to have nothing to do with resting one hand on the rail, and sustaining herself with the other passed through his arm, while she was altogether intent upon the scene below. The ex-military gentleman, the head of the party, and apparently her kinsman, had stepped aside without her knowing, and she had unwittingly taken Mr. Arbuton's arm. So much was clear to him, but what he was to do was not so plain. It did not seem quite his place to tell her of her mistake, and yet it seemed a piece of unfairness not to do so. To leave the matter alone, however, was the simplest, safest, and pleasantest; for the pressure of the pretty figure lightly thrown upon his arm had something agreeably confiding and appealing in it. So he waited till the young lady, turning to him for some response, discovered her error, and disengaged herself with a face of mingled horror and amusement. Even then he had no inspiration. To speak of the mistake in tones of compliment would have been grossly out of place; an explanation was needless; and to her murmured excuses, he could only bow silently. She flitted into the cabin, and he walked away, leaving the Indians to stagger ashore as they might. His arm seemed still to sustain that elastic weight, and a voice haunted his ear with the words, "A pair of disappointed lovers, I suppose"; and still more awkward and stupid he felt his own part in the affair to be; though at the same time he was not without some obscure resentment of the young girl's mistake as an intrusion upon him.

It was late twilight when the boat reached Tadoussac, and ran into a sheltered cove under the shadow of uplands on which a quaint village perched and dispersed itself on a country road in summer cottages; above these in turn rose loftier heights of barren sand or rock, with here and there a rank of sickly pines dying along their sterility. It had been harsh and cold all day when the boat moved, for it was running full in the face of the northeast; the river had widened almost to a sea, growing more and more desolate, with a few lonely islands breaking its expanse, and the shores sinking lower and lower till, near Tadoussac, they rose a little in flat-topped bluffs thickly overgrown with stunted evergreens. Here, into the vast low-walled breadth of the St. Lawrence, a dark stream, narrowly bordered by rounded heights of rock, steals down from the north out of regions of gloomy and ever-during solitude. This is the Saguenay; and in the cold evening light under which the traveller approaches its mouth, no landscape could look more forlorn than that of Tadoussac, where early in the sixteenth century the French traders fixed their first post, and where still the oldest church north of Florida is standing.

The steamer lies here five hours, and supper was no sooner over than the passengers went ashore in the gathering dusk. Mr. Arbuton, guarding his distance as usual, went too, with a feeling of surprise at his own concession to the popular impulse. He was not without a desire to see the old church, wondering in a half-compassionate way what such a bit of American antiquity would look like; and he had perceived since the little embarrassment at Cacouna that he was a discomfort to the young lady involved by it. He had caught no glimpse of her till supper, and then she had briefly supped with an air of such studied unconsciousness of his presence that it was plain she was thinking of her mistake every moment. "Well, I'll leave her the freedom of the boat while we stay," thought Mr. Arbuton as he went ashore. He had not the least notion whither the road led, but like the rest he followed it up through the village, and on among the cottages which seemed for the most part empty, and so down a gloomy ravine, in the bottom of which, far beneath the tremulous rustic bridge, he heard the mysterious crash and fall of an unseen torrent. Before him towered the shadowy hills up into the starless night; he thrilled with a sense of the loneliness and remoteness,

W. D. Howells

and he had a formless wish that some one qualified by the proper associations and traditions were there to share the satisfaction he felt in the whole effect. At the same instant he was once more aware of that delicate pressure, that weight so lightly, sweetly borne upon his arm. It startled him, and again he followed the road, which with a sudden turn brought him in sight of a hotel and in sound of a bowling-alley, and therein young ladies' cackle and laughter, and he wondered a little scornfully who could be spending the summer there. A bay of the river loftily shut in by rugged hills lay before him, and on the shore, just above high-tide, stood what a wandering shadow told him was the ancient church of Tadoussac. The windows were faintly tinged with red as from a single taper burning within, and but that the elements were a little too bare and simple for one so used to the rich effects of the Old World, Mr. Arbuton might have been touched by the vigil which this poor chapel was still keeping after three hundred years in the heart of that gloomy place. While he stood at least tolerating its appeal, he heard voices of people talking in the obscurity near the church door, which they seemed to have been vainly trying for entrance.

"Pity we can't see the inside, isn't it?"

"Yes; but I am so glad to see any of it. Just think of its having been built in the seventeenth century!"

"Uncle Jack would enjoy it, wouldn't he?"

"O yes, poor Uncle Jack! I feel somehow as if I were cheating him out of it. He ought to be here in my place. But I *do* like it; and, Dick, I don't know what I can ever say or do to you and Fanny for bringing me."

"Well, Kitty, postpone the subject till you can think of the right thing. We're in no hurry."

Mr. Arbuton heard a shaking of the door, as of a final attempt upon it, before retreat, and then the voices faded into inarticulate sounds in the darkness. They were the voices, he easily recognized, of the young lady who had taken his arm, and of that kinsman of hers, as she seemed to be. He blamed himself for having not only overheard them, but for desiring to hear more of their talk, and he resolved to follow them back to the boat at a discreet distance. But they loitered so at every point, or he unwittingly made such haste, that he had overtaken them as they entered the lane between the outlying cottages, and he could not help being privy to their talk again.

"Well, it may be old, Kitty, but I don't think it's lively."

"It *isn't* exactly a whirl of excitement, I must confess."

"It's the deadliest place I ever saw. Is that a swing in front of that cottage? No, it's a gibbet. Why, they've all got 'em! I suppose they're for the summer tenants at the close of the season. What a rush there would be for them if the boat should happen to go off and leave her passengers!"

Mr. Arbuton thought this rather a coarse kind of drolling, and strengthened himself anew in his resolution to avoid those people.

They now came in sight of the steamer, where in the cove she lay illumined with all her lamps, and through every window and door and crevice was bursting with the ruddy light. Her brilliancy contrasted vividly with the obscurity and loneliness of the shore where a few lights glimmered in the village houses, and under the porch of the village store some desolate idlers— *habitans* and half-breeds—had clubbed their miserable leisure. Beyond the steamer yawned the wide vacancy of the greater river, and out of this gloomed the course of the Saguenay.

"O, I hate to go on board!" said the young lady. "Do you think he's got back yet? It's perfect misery to meet him."

"Never mind, Kitty. He probably thinks you didn't mean anything by it. *I* don't believe you would have taken his arm if you hadn't supposed it was mine, *any* way."

She made no answer to this, as if too much overcome by the true state of the case to be troubled by its perversion. Mr. Arbuton, following them on board, felt himself in the unpleasant character of persecutor, some one to be shunned and escaped by every maneuver possible to self-respect. He was to be the means, it appeared, of spoiling the enjoyment of the voyage for one who, he inferred, had not often the opportunity of such enjoyment. He had a willingness that she should think well and not ill of him; and then at the bottom of all was a sentiment of superiority, which, if he had given it shape, would have been *noblesse oblige*. Some action was due to himself as a gentleman.

The young lady went to seek the matron of the party, and left her companion at the door of the saloon, wistfully fingering a cigar in one hand, and feeling for a match with the other. Presently he gave himself a clap on the waistcoat which he had found empty, and was turning away, when Mr. Arbuton said, offering his own lighted cigar, "May I be of use to you?"

The other took it with a hearty, "O yes, thank you!" and, with many inarticulate murmurs of satisfaction, lighted his cigar, and returned Mr. Arbuton's with a brisk, half-military bow.

Mr. Arbuton looked at him narrowly a moment. "I'm afraid," he said abruptly, "that I've most unluckily been the cause of annoyance to one of the ladies of your party. It isn't a thing to apologize for, and I hardly know how to say that I hope, if she's not already forgotten the matter, she'll do so." Saying this, Mr. Arbuton, by an impulse which he would have been at a loss to explain, offered his card.

His action had the effect of frankness, and the other took it for cordiality. He drew near a lamp, and looked at the name and street address on the card, and then said, "Ah, of Boston! *My* name is Ellison; I'm of Milwaukee, Wisconsin." And he laughed a free, trustful laugh of good companionship. "Why yes, my cousin's been tormenting herself about her mistake the whole afternoon; but of course it's all right, you know. Bless my heart! it was the most natural thing in the world. Have you been ashore? There's a good deal of repose about Tadoussac, now; but it must be a lively place in winter! Such a cheerful lookout from these cottages, or that hotel over yonder! We went over to see if we could get into the little old church; the purser told me there are some lead tablets there, left by Jacques Cartier's men, you know, and dug up in the neighborhood. I don't think it's likely, and I'm bearing up very well under the disappointment of not getting in. I've done my duty by the antiquities of the place; and now I don't care how soon we are off."

Colonel Ellison was talking in the kindness of his heart to change the subject which the younger gentleman had introduced, in the belief, which would scarcely have pleased the other, that he was much embarrassed. His good-nature went still further; and when his cousin returned presently, with Mrs. Ellison, he presented Mr. Arbuton to the ladies, and then thoughtfully made Mrs. Ellison walk up and down the deck with him for the exercise she would not take ashore, that the others might be left to deal with their vexation alone.

"I am very sorry, Miss Ellison," said Mr. Arbuton, "to have been the means of a mistake to you to-day."

"And I was dreadfully ashamed to make you the victim of my blunder," answered Miss Ellison penitently; and a little silence ensued. Then as if she had suddenly been able to alienate the case, and see it apart from herself in its unmanageable absurdity, she broke into a confiding laugh, very like her cousin's, and said, "Why, it's one of the most hopeless things I ever heard of. I don't see what in the world can be done about it."

"It *is* rather a difficult matter, and I'm not prepared to say myself. Before I make up my mind I should like it to happen again."

W. D. Howells

Mr. Arbuton had no sooner made this speech, which he thought neat, than he was vexed with himself for having made it, since nothing was further from his purpose than a flirtation. But the dark, vicinity, the young girl's prettiness, the apparent freshness and reliance on his sympathy from which her frankness came, were too much: he tried to congeal again, and ended in some feebleness about the scenery, which was indeed very lonely and wild, after the boat started up the Saguenay, leaving the few lights of Tadoussac to blink and fail behind her. He had an absurd sense of being alone in the world there with the young lady; and he suffered himself to enjoy the situation, which was as perfectly safe as anything could be. He and Miss Ellison had both come on from Niagara, it seemed, and they talked of that place, she consciously withholding the fact that she had noticed Mr. Arbuton there; they had both come down the Rapids of the St. Lawrence, and they had both stopped a day in Montreal. These common experiences gave them a surprising interest for each other, which was enhanced by the discovery that their experiences differed thereafter, and that whereas she had passed three days at Quebec, he, as we know, had come on directly from Montreal.

"Did you enjoy Quebec very much, Miss Ellison?"

"O yes, indeed! It's a beautiful old town, with everything in it that I had always read about and never expected to see. You know it's a walled city."

"Yes. But I confess I had forgotten it till this morning. Did you find it all that you expected a walled city to be?"

"More, if possible. There were some Boston people with us there, and they said it was exactly like Europe. They fairly sighed over it, and it seemed to remind them of pretty nearly everything they had seen abroad. They were just married."

"Did that make Quebec look like Europe?"

"No, but I suppose it made them willing to see it in the

pleasantest light. Mrs. March—that was their name—wouldn't allow me to say that *I* enjoyed Quebec, because if I hadn't seen Europe, I *could*n't properly enjoy it. 'You may *think* you enjoy it,' she was always saying, 'but that's merely fancy.' Still I cling to my delusion. But I don't know whether I cared more for Quebec, or the beautiful little villages in the country all about it. The whole landscape looks just like a dream of 'Evangeline.'"

"Indeed! I must certainly stop at Quebec. I should like to see an American landscape that put one in mind of anything. What can your imagination do for the present scenery?"

"I don't think it needs any help from me," replied the young girl, as if the tone of her companion had patronized and piqued her. She turned as she spoke and looked up the sad, lonely river. The moon was making its veiled face seen through the gray heaven, and touching the black stream with hints of melancholy light. On either hand the uninhabitable shore rose in desolate grandeur, friendless heights of rock with a thin covering of pines seen in dim outline along their tops and deepening into the solid dark of hollows and ravines upon their sides. The cry of some wild bird struck through the silence of which the noise of the steamer had grown to be a part, and echoed away to nothing. Then from the saloon there came on a sudden the notes of a song; and Miss Ellison led the way within, where most of the other passengers were grouped about the piano. The English girl with the corn-colored hair sat, in ravishing picture, at the instrument, and the commonish man and his very plain wife were singing with heavenly sweetness together.

"Isn't it beautiful!" said Miss Ellison. "How nice it must be to be able to do such things!"

"Yes? do you think so? It's rather public," answered her companion.

When the English people had ended, a grave, elderly Canadian gentleman sat down to give what he believed a comic song, and sent everybody disconsolate to bed.

"Well, Kitty?" cried Mrs. Ellison, shutting herself inside the young lady's state-room a moment.

"Well, Fanny?"

"Isn't he handsome?"

"He is, indeed."

"Is he nice?"

"I don't know."

"Sweet?"

"*Ice*-cream," said Kitty, and placidly let herself be kissed an enthusiastic good-night. Before Mrs. Ellison slept she wished to ask her husband one question.

"What is it?"

"Should you want Kitty to marry a Bostonian? They say Bostonians are so cold."

"What Bostonian has been asking Kitty to marry him?"

"O, how spiteful you are! I didn't say any had. But if there should?"

"Then it'll be time to think about it. You've married Kitty right and left to everybody who's looked at her since we left Niagara, and I've worried myself to death investigating the character of her husbands. Now I'm not going to do it any longer,—till she has an offer."

"Very well. *You* can depreciate your own cousin, if you like.

But I know what *I* shall do. I shall let her wear all my best things. How fortunate it is, Richard, that we're exactly of a size! O, I am so glad we brought Kitty along! If she should marry and settle down in Boston—no, I hope she could get her husband to live in New York—"

"Go on, go on, my dear!" cried Colonel Ellison, with a groan of despair. "Kitty has talked twenty-five minutes with this young man about the hotels and steamboats, and of course he'll be round to-morrow morning asking my consent to marry her as soon as we can get to a justice of the peace. My hair is gradually turning gray, and I shall be bald before my time; but I don't mind that if you find any pleasure in these little hallucinations of yours. *Go* on!"

II

MRS. ELLISON'S LITTLE MANEUVRE

The next morning our tourists found themselves at rest in Ha-Ha Bay, at the head of navigation for the larger steamers. The long line of sullen hills had fallen away, and the morning sun shone warm on what in a friendlier climate would have been a very lovely landscape. The bay was an irregular oval, with shores that rose in bold but not lofty heights on one side, while on the other lay a narrow plain with two villages clinging about the road that followed the crescent beach, and lifting each the slender tin-clad spire of its church to sparkle in the sun.

At the head of the bay was a mountainous top, and along its waters were masses of rocks, gayly painted with lichens and stained with metallic tints of orange and scarlet. The unchanging growth of stunted pines was the only forest in sight, though Ha-Ha Bay is a famous lumbering port, and some schooners now lay there receiving cargoes of odorous pine plank. The steamboat-wharf was all astir with the liveliest toil and leisure. The boat was taking on wood, which was brought in wheelbarrows to the top of the steep, smooth gangway-planking, where the *habitant* in charge planted his broad feet for the downward slide, and was hurled aboard more or less *en masse* by the fierce velocity of his heavy-laden wheelbarrow. Amidst the confusion and hazard of this feat a procession of other habitans marched aboard, each one bearing under his arm a coffin-shaped wooden box. The rising fear of

Colonel Ellison, that these boxes represented the loss of the whole infant population of Ha-Ha Bay, was checked by the reflection that the region could not have produced so many children, and calmed altogether by the purser, who said that they were full of huckleberries, and that Colonel Ellison could have as many as he liked for fifteen cents a bushel. This gave him a keen sense of the poverty of the land, and he bought of the boys who came aboard such abundance of wild red raspberries, in all manner of birch-bark canoes and goblets and cornucopias, that he was obliged to make presents of them to the very dealers whose stock he had exhausted, and he was in treaty with the local half-wit—very fine, with a hunchback, and a massive wen on one side of his head—to take charity in the wild fruits of his native province, when the crowd about him was gently opened by a person who advanced with a flourishing bow and a sprightly "Good morning, good morning, sir!" "How do you do?" asked Colonel Ellison; but the other, intent on business, answered, "I am the only person at Ha-Ha Bay who speaks English, and I have come to ask if you would not like to make a promenade in my horse and buggy upon the mountain before breakfast. You shall be gone as long as you will for one shilling and sixpence. I will show you all that there is to be seen about the place, and the beautiful view of the bay from the top of the mountain. But it is elegant, you know, I can assure you."

The speaker was so fluent of his English, he had such an audacious, wide-branching mustache, such a twinkle in his left eye,—which wore its lid in a careless, slouching fashion,—that the heart of man naturally clove to him; and Colonel Ellison agreed on the spot to make the proposed promenade, for himself and both his ladies, of whom he went joyfully in search. He found them at the stern of the boat, admiring the wild scenery, and looking

"Fresh as the morn and as the season fair."

He was not a close observer, and of his wife's wardrobe he had the ignorance of a good husband, who, as soon as the pang of

W. D. Howells

paying for her dresses is past, forgets whatever she has; but he could not help seeing that some gayeties of costume which he had dimly associated with his wife now enhanced the charms of his cousin's nice little face and figure. A scarf of lively hue carelessly tied about the throat to keep off the morning chill, a prettier ribbon, a more stylish jacket than Miss Ellison owned,—what do I know?—an air of preparation for battle, caught the colonel's eye, and a conscious red stole responsive into Kitty's cheek.

"Kitty," said he, "don't you let yourself be made a goose of."

"I hope she won't—by *you*!" retorted his wife, "and I'll thank you, Colonel Ellison, not to be a Betty, whatever you are. I don't think it's manly to be always noticing ladies' clothes."

"Who said anything about clothes?" demanded the colonel, taking his stand upon the letter.

"Well, don't *you*, at any rate. Yes, I'd like to ride, of all things; and we've time enough, for breakfast isn't ready till half past eight. Where's the carriage?"

The only English scholar at Ha-Ha Bay had taken the light wraps of the ladies and was moving off with them. "This way, this way," he said, waving his hand towards a larger number of vehicles on the shore than could have been reasonably attributed to Ha-Ha Bay. "I hope you won't object to having another passenger with you? There's plenty of room for all. He seems a very nice, gentlemanly person," said he, with a queer, patronizing graciousness which he had no doubt caught from his English patrons.

"The more the merrier," answered Colonel Ellison, and "Not in the least!" said his wife, not meaning the proverb. Her eye had swept the whole array of vehicles and had found them all empty, save one, in which she detected the blamelessly coated back of Mr. Arbuton. But I ought perhaps to explain Mrs. Ellison's motives better than they can be made to appear in her conduct. She cared nothing for Mr. Arbuton; and she had no logical wish to see Kitty in love with him. But here were two young people thrown somewhat romantically together; Mrs. Ellison was a born match-maker, and to have refrained from promoting their better acquaintance in the interest of abstract matrimony was what never could have entered into her thought or desire. Her whole being closed for the time about this purpose; her heart, always warm towards Kitty,—whom she admired with a sort of generous frenzy,—expanded with all kinds of lovely designs; in a word, every dress she had she would instantly have bestowed upon that worshipful creature who was capable of adding another marriage to the world. I hope the reader finds nothing vulgar or unbecoming in this, for I do not; it was an enthusiasm, pure and simple, a beautiful and unselfish abandon; and I am sure men ought to be sorry that they are not worthier to be favored by it. Ladies have often to lament in the midst of their finesse that, really, no man is deserving the fate they devote themselves to prepare for him, or, in other words, that women cannot marry women.

I am not going to be so rash as try to depict Mrs. Ellison's arts, for then, indeed, I should make her appear the clumsy conspirator she was not, and should merely convict myself of ignorance of such matters. Whether Mr. Arbuton was ever aware of them, I am not sure: as a man he was, of course, obtuse and blind; but then, on the other hand, he had seen far more of the world than Mrs. Ellison, and she may have been clear as day to him. Probably, though, he did not detect any design; he could not have conceived of such a thing in a person with whom he had been so irregularly made acquainted, and to whom he felt himself so hopelessly superior. A film of ice such as in autumn you find casing the still pools early in the frosty mornings had gathered upon his manner over night; but it thawed under the greetings of the others, and he jumped actively out of the vehicle to offer the ladies their choice of seats. When all was arranged he found himself at Mrs. Ellison's side, for Kitty had somewhat eagerly climbed to the front seat with the colonel. In these circumstances it was pure zeal that sustained Mrs. Ellison in the flattering constancy with which

W. D. Howells

she babbled on to Mr. Arbuton and refrained from openly resenting Kitty's contumacy.

As the wagon began to ascend the hill, the road was so rough that the springs smote together with pitiless jolts, and the ladies uttered some irrepressible moans. "Never mind, my dear," said the colonel, turning about to his wife, "we've got all the English there is at Ha-Ha Bay, any way." Whereupon the driver gave him a wink of sudden liking and good-fellowship. At the same time his tongue was loosed, and he began to talk of himself. "You see my dog, how he leaps at the horse's nose? He is a moose-dog, and keeps himself in practice of catching the moose by the nose. You ought to come in the hunting season. I could furnish you with Indians and everything you need to hunt with. I am a dealer in wild beasts, you know, and I must keep prepared to take them."

"Wild beasts?"

"Yes, for Barnum and the other showmen. I deal in deer, wolf, bear, beaver, moose, cariboo, wild-cat, link—"

"What?"

"Link—link! You say deer for deers, and link for lynx, don't you?"

"Certainly," answered the unblushing colonel. "Are there many link about here?"

"Not many, and they are a very expensive animal. I have been shamefully treated in a link that I have sold to a Boston show-man. It was a difficult beast to take; bit my Indian awfully; and Mr. Doolittle would not give the price he promised."

"What an outrage!"

"Yes, but it was not so bad as it might have been. He wanted the money back afterwards; the link died in about two weeks," said the dealer in wild animals, with a smile that curled his mustache into his ears, and a glance at Colonel Ellison. "He may have been bruised, I suppose. He may have been homesick. Perhaps he was never a very strong link. The link is a curious animal, miss," he said to Kitty, in conclusion.

They had been slowly climbing the mountain road, from which, on either hand, the pasturelands fell away in long, irregular knolls and hollows. The tops were quite barren, but in the little vales, despite the stones, a short grass grew very thick and tenderly green, and groups of kine tinkled their soft bells in a sweet, desultory assonance as they cropped the herbage. Below, the bay filled the oval of the hills with its sunny expanse, and the white steamer, where she lay beside the busy wharf, and the black lumber-ships, gave their variety to the pretty scene, which was completed by the picturesque villages on the shore. It was a very simple sight, but somehow very touching, as if the soft spectacle were but a respite from desolation and solitude; as indeed it was.

Mr. Arbuton must have been talking of travel elsewhere, for now he said to Mrs. Ellison, "This looks like a bit of Norway; the bay yonder might very well be a fjord of the Northern sea."

Mrs. Ellison murmured her sense of obligation to the bay, the fjord, and Mr. Arbuton, for their complaisance, and Kitty remembered that he had somewhat snubbed her the night before for attributing any suggestive grace to the native scenery. "Then you've really found something in an American landscape. I suppose we ought to congratulate it," she said, in smiling enjoyment of her triumph.

The colonel looked at her with eyes of humorous question; Mrs. Ellison looked blank; and Mr. Arbuton, having quite forgotten what he had said to provoke this comment now, looked puzzled and answered nothing: for he had this trait also in common with the sort of Englishman for whom he was taken, that he never helped out your conversational venture, but if he failed to respond inwardly, left you with your unaccepted remark upon your hands, as it were. In his silence, Kitty fell a prey to very evil thoughts of him, for it made her harmless sally look like a blundering attack upon him. But just then the driver came to her rescue; he said, "Gentlemen and ladies, this is the end of the mountain promenade," and, turning his horse's head, drove rapidly back to the village.

At the foot of the hill they came again to the church, and his passengers wanted to get out and look into it. "O certainly," said he, "it isn't finished yet, but you can say as many prayers as you like in it."

The church was decent and clean, like most Canadian churches, and at this early hour there was a good number of the villagers at their devotions. The lithographic pictures of the stations to Calvary were, of course, on its walls, and there was the ordinary tawdriness of paint and carving about the high altar.

"I don't like to see these things," said Mrs. Ellison. "It really seems to savor of idolatry. Don't you think so, Mr. Arbuton?"

"Well, I don't know. I doubt if they're the sort of people to be hurt by it."

"They need a good stout faith in cold climates, I can tell you," said the colonel. "It helps to keep them warm. The broad church would be too full of draughts up here. They want something snug and tight. Just imagine one of these poor devils listening to a liberal sermon about birds and fruits and flowers and beautiful sentiments, and then driving home over the hills with the mercury thirty degrees below zero! He couldn't stand it."

"Yes, yes, certainly," said Mr. Arbuton, and looked about him with an eye of cold, uncompassionate inspection, as if he were trying it by a standard of taste, and, on the whole, finding the poor little church vulgar.

When they mounted to their places again, the talk fell entirely to the colonel, who, as his wont was, got what information he could out of the driver. It appeared, in spite of his theory, that they were not all good Catholics at Ha-Ha Bay. "This chap, for example," said the Frenchman, touching himself on the breast and using the slang he must have picked up from American travellers, "is no Catholic,—not much! He has made too many studies to care for religion. There's a large French party, sir, in Canada, that's opposed to the priests and in favor of annexation."

He satisfied the colonel's utmost curiosity, discoursing, as he drove by the log-built cottages which were now and then sheathed in birch-bark, upon the local affairs, and the character and history of such of his fellow-villagers as they met. He knew the pretty girls upon the street and saluted them by name, interrupting himself with these courtesies in the lecture he was giving the colonel on life at Ha-Ha Bay. There was only one brick house (which he had built himself, but had been obliged to sell in a season unfavorable for wild beasts), and the other edifices dropped through the social scale to some picturesque barns thatched with straw. These he excused to his Americans, but added that the ungainly thatch was sometimes useful in saving the lives of the cattle toward the end of an unusually long, hard winter.

"And the people," asked the colonel, "what do they do in the winter to pass the time?"

"Draw the wood, smoke the pipe, court the ladies.—But wouldn't you like to see the inside of one of our poor cottages? I shall be very proud to have you look at mine, and to have you drink a glass of milk from my cows. I am sorry that I cannot offer you brandy, but there's none to be bought in the place."

"Don't speak of it! For an eye-opener there is nothing like a glass of milk," gayly answered the colonel.

They entered the best room of the house,—wide, low-ceiled, dimly lit by two small windows, and fortified against the winter by a huge Canada stove of cast-iron. It was rude but neat, and had an air of decent comfort. Through the window appeared a very little vegetable garden with a border of the hardiest flowers. "The large beans there," explained the host, "are for soup and coffee. My corn," he said, pointing out some rows of dwarfish maize, "has escaped the early August frosts, and so I expect to have some roasting-ears yet this summer."

"Well, it isn't exactly what you'd call an inviting climate, is it?" asked the colonel.

The Canadian seemed a hard little man, but he answered now with a kind of pathos, "It's cruel! I came here when it was all bush. Twenty years I have lived here, and it has not been worth while. If it was to do over again, I should rather not live anywhere. I was born in Quebec," he said, as if to explain that he was used to mild climates, and began to tell of some events of his life at Ha-Ha Bay. "I wish you were going to stay here awhile with me. You wouldn't find it so bad in the summer-time, I can assure you. There are bears in the bush, sir," he said to the colonel, "and you might easily kill one."

"But then I should be helping to spoil your trade in wild beasts," replied the colonel, laughing.

Mr. Arbuton looked like one who might be very tired of this. He made no sign of interest either in the early glooms and privations or the summer bears of Ha-Ha Bay. He sat in the quaint parlor, with his hat on his knee, in the decorous and patient attitude of a gentleman making a call.

He had no feeling, Kitty said to herself; but that is a matter about which we can easily be wrong. It was rather to be said of Mr. Arbuton that he had always shrunk from knowledge of things outside of a very narrow world, and that he had not a ready imagination. Moreover, he had a personal dislike, as I may call it, of poverty; and he did not enjoy this poverty as she did, because it was strange and suggestive, though doubtless he would have done as much to relieve distress.

"Rather too much of his autobiography," he said to Kitty, as he waited outside the door with her, while the Canadian quieted his dog, which was again keeping himself in practice of catching the moose by making vicious leaps at the horse's nose. "The egotism of that kind of people is always so aggressive. But I suppose he's in the habit of throwing himself upon the sympathy of summer visitors in this way. You can't offer a man so little as shilling and sixpence who's taken you into his confidence. Did you find enough that was novel in his place to justify him in bringing us here, Miss Ellison?" he asked with an air he had of taking you of course to be of his mind, and which equally offended you whether you were so or not.

Every face that they had seen in their drive had told its pathetic story to Kitty; every cottage that they passed she had entered in thought, and dreamed out its humble drama. What their host had said gave breath and color to her fancies of the struggle of life there, and she was startled and shocked when this cold doubt was cast upon the sympathetic tints of her picture. She did not know what to say at first; she looked at Mr. Arbuton with a sudden glance of embarrassment and trouble; then she answered, "I was very much interested. I don't agree with you, I believe"; which, when she heard it, seemed a resentful little speech, and made her willing for some occasion to soften its effect. But nothing occurred to her during the brief drive back to the boat, save the fact that the morning air was delicious.

"Yes, but rather cool," said Mr. Arbuton, whose feelings apparently had not needed any balm; and the talk fell again to the others.

On the pier he helped her down from the wagon, for the colonel was intent on something the driver was saying, and then offered his hand to Mrs. Ellison.

She sprang from her place, but stumbled slightly, and when

W. D. Howells

she touched the ground, "I believe I turned my foot a little," she said with a laugh. "It's nothing, of course," and fainted in his arms.

Kitty gave a cry of alarm, and the next instant the colonel had relieved Mr. Arbuton. It was a scene, and nothing could have annoyed him more than this tumult which poor Mrs. Ellison's misfortune occasioned among the bystanding habitans and deck-hands, and the passengers eagerly craning forward over the bulwarks, and running ashore to see what the matter was. Few men know just how to offer those little offices of helpfulness which such emergencies demand, and Mr. Arbuton could do nothing after he was rid of his burden; he hovered anxiously and uselessly about, while Mrs. Ellison was carried to an airy position on the bow of the boat, where in a few minutes he had the great satisfaction of seeing her open her eyes. It was not the moment for him to speak, and he walked somewhat guiltily away with the dispersing crowd.

Mrs. Ellison addressed her first words to pale Kitty at her side. "You can have all my things, now," she said, as if it were a clause in her will, and perhaps it had been her last thought before unconsciousness.

"Why, Fanny," cried Kitty, with an hysterical laugh, "you're not going to die! A sprained ankle isn't fatal!"

"No; but I've heard that a person with a sprained ankle can't put their foot to the ground for weeks; and I shall only want a dressing-gown, you know, to lie on the sofa in." With that, Mrs. Ellison placed her hand tenderly on Kitty's head, like a mother wondering what will become of a helpless child during her disability; in fact she was mentally weighing the advantages of her wardrobe, which Kitty would now fully enjoy, against the loss of the friendly strategy which she would now lack. Helpless to decide the matter, she heaved a sigh.

"But, Fanny, you won't expect to travel in a dressing-gown."

"Indeed, I wish I knew whether I *could* travel in *anything* or not. But the next twenty-four hours will show. If it swells up, I shall have to rest awhile at Quebec; and if it doesn't, there may be something internal. I've read of accidents when the person thought they were perfectly well and comfortable, and the first thing they knew they were in a very dangerous state. That's the worst of these internal injuries: you never can tell. Not that I think there's anything of that kind the matter with me. But a few days' rest won't do any harm, whatever happens; the stores in Quebec are quite as good and a little cheaper than in Montreal; and I could go about in a carriage, you know, and put in the time as well in one place as the other. I'm sure we could get on very pleasantly there; and the colonel needn't be home for a month yet. I suppose that I could hobble into the stores on a crutch."

Whilst Mrs. Ellison's monologue ran on with scarcely a break from Kitty, her husband was gone to fetch her a cup of tea and such other light refreshment as a lady may take after a swoon. When he returned she bethought herself of Mr. Arbuton, who, having once come back to see if all was going well, had vanished again.

"Why, our friend Boston is bearing up under his share of the morning's work like a hero—or a lady with a sprained ankle," said the colonel as he arranged the provision. "To see the havoc he's making in the ham and eggs and chiccory is to be convinced that there is no appetizer like regret for the sufferings of others."

"Why, and here's poor Kitty not had a bite yet!" cried Mrs. Ellison. "Kitty, go off at once and get your breakfast. Put on my—"

"O, *don't*, Fanny, or I can't go; and I'm really very hungry."

"Well, I won't then," said Mrs. Ellison, seeing the rainy cloud in Kitty's eyes. "Go just as you are, and don't mind me." And so Kitty went, gathering courage at every pace, and sitting down opposite Mr. Arbuton with a vivid color to be sure, but otherwise lion-bold. He had been upbraiding the stars that had thrust him further and further at every step into the intimacy of these people, as he called them to himself. It was just twenty-four hours, he reflected, since he had met them, and resolved to have nothing to do with them, and in that time the young lady had brought him under the necessity of apologizing for a blunder of her own; he had played the eavesdropper to her talk; he had sentimentalized the midnight hour with her; they had all taken a morning ride together; and he had ended by having Mrs. Ellison sprain her ankle and faint in his arms. It was outrageous; and what made it worse was that decency obliged him to take henceforth a regretful, deprecatory attitude towards Mrs. Ellison, whom he liked least among these people. So he sat vindictively eating an enormous breakfast, in a sort of angry abstraction, from which Kitty's coming roused him to say that he hoped Mrs. Ellison was better.

"O, very much! It's just a sprain."

"A sprain may be a very annoying thing," said Mr. Arbuton dismally. "Miss Ellison," he cried, "I've been nothing but an affliction to your party since I came on board this boat!"

"Do you think evil genius of our party would be too harsh a term?" suggested Kitty.

"Not in the least; it would be a mere euphemism,—base flattery, in fact. Call me something worse."

"I can't think of anything. I must leave you to your own conscience. It was a pity to end our ride in that way; it would have been such a pleasant ride!" And Kitty took heart from his apparent mood to speak of some facts of the morning that had moved her fancy. "What a strange little nest it is up here among these half-thawed hills! and imagine the winter, the fifteen or twenty months of it, they must have every year. I could almost have shed tears over that patch of corn that had escaped the early August frosts. I suppose this is a sort of

Indian summer that we are enjoying now, and that the cold weather will set in after a week or two. My cousin and I thought that Tadoussac was somewhat retired and composed last night, but I'm sure that I shall see it in its true light, as a metropolis, going back. I'm afraid that the turmoil and bustle of Eriecreek, when I get home—"

"Eriecreek?—when you got home?—I thought you lived at Milwaukee."

"O no! It's my cousins who live at Milwaukee. I live at Eriecreek, New York State."

"Oh!" Mr. Arbuton looked blank and not altogether pleased. Milwaukee was bad enough, though he understood that it was largely peopled from New England, and had a great German element, which might account for the fact that these people were not quite barbaric. But this Eriecreek, New York State! "I don't think I've heard of it," he said.

"It's a small place," observed Kitty, "and I believe it isn't noted for anything in particular; it's not even on any railroad. It's in the north-west part of the State."

"Isn't it in the oil-regions?" groped Mr. Arbuton.

"Why, the oil-regions are rather migratory, you know. It used to be in the oil-regions; but the oil was pumped out, and then the oil-regions gracefully withdrew and left the cheese-regions and grape-regions to come back and take possession of the old derricks and the rusty boilers. You might suppose from the appearance of the meadows, that all the boilers that ever blew up had come down in the neighborhood of Eriecreek. And every field has its derrick standing just as the last dollar or the last drop of oil left it."

Mr. Arbuton brought his fancy to bear upon Eriecreek, and wholly failed to conceive of it. He did not like the notion of its being thrust within the range of his knowledge; and he resented its being the home of Miss Ellison, whom he was beginning to accept as a not quite comprehensible yet certainly agreeable fact, though he still had a disposition to cast her off as something incredible. He asked no further about Eriecreek, and presently she rose and went to join her relatives, and he went to smoke his cigar, and to ponder upon the problem presented to him in this young girl from whose locality and conjecturable experiences he was at loss how to infer her as he found her here.

She had a certain self-reliance mingling with an innocent trust of others which Mrs. Isabel March had described to her husband as a charm potent to make everybody sympathetic and good-natured, but which it would not be easy to account for to Mr. Arbuton. In part it was a natural gift, and partly it came from mere ignorance of the world; it was the unsnubbed fearlessness of a heart which did not suspect a sense of social difference in others, or imagine itself misprized for anything but a fault. For such a false conception of her relations to polite society, Kitty's Uncle Jack was chiefly to blame. In the fierce democracy of his revolt from his Virginian traditions he had taught his family that a belief in any save intellectual and moral distinctions was a mean and cruel superstition; he had contrived to fix this idea so deeply in the education of his children, that it gave a coloring to their lives, and Kitty, when her turn came, had the effect of it in the character of those about her. In fact she accepted his extreme theories of equality to a degree that delighted her uncle, who, having held them many years, was growing perhaps a little languid in their tenure and was glad to have his grasp strengthened by her faith. Socially as well as politically Eriecreek was almost a perfect democracy, and there was little in Kitty's circumstances to contradict the doctor's teachings. The brief visits which she had made to Buffalo and Erie, and, since the colonel's marriage, to Milwaukee, had not sufficed to undeceive her; she had never suffered slight save from the ignorant and uncouth; she innocently expected that in people of culture she should always find community of feeling and ideas; and she had met Mr. Arbuton all the more trustfully because as a Bostonian he must be cultivated.

In the secluded life which she led perforce at Eriecreek there was an abundance of leisure, which she bestowed upon books at an age when most girls are sent to school. The doctor had a good taste of an old-fashioned kind in literature, and he had a library pretty well stocked with the elderly English authors, poets and essayists and novelists, and here and there an historian, and these Kitty read childlike, liking them at the time in a certain way, and storing up in her mind things that she did not understand for the present, but whose beauty and value dawned upon her from time to time, as she grew older. But of far more use and pleasure to her than these now somewhat mouldy classics were the more modern books of her cousin Charles,—that pride and hope of his father's heart, who had died the year before she came to Eriecreek. He was named after her own father, and it was as if her Uncle Jack found both his son and his brother in her again. When her taste for reading began to show itself in force, the old man one day unlocked a certain bookcase in a little upper room, and gave her the key, saying, with a broken pride and that queer Virginian pomp which still clung to him, "This was my son's, who would one day have been a great writer; now it is yours." After that the doctor would pick up the books out of this collection which Kitty was reading and had left lying about the rooms, and look into them a little way. Sometimes he fell asleep over them; sometimes when he opened on a page pencilled with marginal notes, he would put the volume gently down and go very quickly out of the room.

"Kitty, I reckon you'd better not leave poor Charley's books around where Uncle Jack can get at them," one of the girls, Virginia or Rachel, would say; "I don't believe he cares much for those writers, and the sight of the books just tries him." So Kitty kept the books, and herself for the most part with them, in the upper chamber which had been Charles Ellison's room, and where, amongst the witnesses of the dead boy's ambitious dreams, she grew dreamer herself and seemed to inherit with his earthly place his own fine and gentle spirit.

W. D. Howells

The doctor, as his daughter suggested, did not care much for the modern authors in whom his son had delighted. Like many another simple and pure-hearted man, he thought that since Pope there had been no great poet but Byron, and he could make nothing out of Tennyson and Browning, or the other contemporary English poets. Amongst the Americans he had a great respect for Whittier, but he preferred Lowell to the rest because he had written The Biglow Papers, and he never would allow that the last series was half so good as the first. These and the other principal poets of our nation and language Kitty inherited from her cousin, as well as a full stock of the contemporary novelists and romancers, whom she liked better than the poets on the whole. She had also the advantage of the magazines and reviews which used to come to him, and the house over-flowed with newspapers of every kind, from the Eriecreek Courier to the New York Tribune. What with the coming and going of the eccentric visitors, and this continual reading, and her rides about the country with her Uncle Jack, Kitty's education, such as it was, went on very actively and with the effect, at least, to give her a great liveliness of mind and several decided opinions. Where it might have warped her out of natural simplicity, and made her conceited, the keen and wholesome airs which breathed continually in the Ellison household came in to restore her. There was such kindness in this discipline, that she never could remember when it wounded her; it was part of the gayety of those times when she would sit down with the girls, and they took up some work together, and rattled on in a free, wild, racy talk, with an edge of satire for whoever came near, a fantastic excess in its drollery, and just a touch of native melancholy tingeing it. The last queer guest, some neighborhood gossip, some youthful folly or pretentiousness of Kitty's, some trait of their own, some absurdity of the boys if they happened to be at home, and came lounging in, were the themes out of which they contrived such jollity as never was, save when in Uncle Jack's presence they fell upon some characteristic action or theory of his and turned it into endless ridicule.

But of such people, of such life, Mr. Arbuton could have made nothing if he had known them. In many things he was an excellent person, and greatly to be respected for certain qualities. He was very sincere; his mind had a singular purity and rectitude; he was a scrupulously just person so far as he knew. He had traits that would have fitted him very well for the career he had once contemplated, and he had even made some preliminary studies for the ministry. But the very generosity of his creed perplexed him, his mislikers said; contending that he could never have got on with the mob of the redeemed. "Arbuton," said a fat young fellow, the supposed wit of the class, "thinks there *are* persons of low extraction in heaven; but he doesn't like the idea." And Mr. Arbuton did not like the speaker very well, either, nor any of his poorer fellow-students, whose gloveless and unfashionable poverty, and meagre board and lodgings, and general hungry dependence upon pious bequests and neighborhood kindnesses, offended his instincts. "So he's given it up, has he?" moralized the same wit, upon his retirement. "If Arbuton could have been a divinely commissioned apostle to the best society, and been obliged to save none but well-connected, old-established, and cultivated souls, he might have gone into the ministry." This was a coarse construction of the truth, but it was not altogether a perversion. It was long ago that he had abandoned the thought of the ministry, and he had since travelled, and read law, and become a man of society and of clubs; but he still kept the traits that had seemed to make his vocation clear. On the other hand he kept the prejudices that were imagined to have disqualified him. He was an exclusive by training and by instinct. He gave ordinary humanity credit for a certain measure of sensibility, and it is possible that if he had known more kinds of men, he would have recognized merits and excellences which did not now exist for him; but I do not think he would have liked them. His doubt of these Western people was the most natural, if not the most justifiable thing in the world, and for Kitty, if he could have known all about her, I do not see how he could have believed in her at all. As it was, he went in search of her party, when he had smoked his cigar, and found them on the forward promenade. She had left him in quite a lenient mood, although, as she perceived with amusement, he had done nothing to merit it, except give her cousin a sprained ankle. At the moment of his reappearance, Mrs. Ellison had been telling Kitty that she thought it was beginning to swell a little, and so it could not be anything internal; and Kitty had understood that she meant her ankle as well as if she had said so, and had sorrowed and rejoiced over her, and the colonel had been inculpated for the whole affair. This made Mr. Arbuton's excuses rather needless, though they were most graciously received.

III

ON THE WAY BACK TO QUEBEC

By this time the boat was moving down the river, and every one was alive to the scenery. The procession of the pine-clad, rounded heights on either shore began shortly after Ha-Ha Bay had disappeared behind a curve, and it hardly ceased, save at one point, before the boat re-entered the St. Lawrence. The shores of the stream are almost uninhabited. The hills rise from the water's edge, and if ever a narrow vale divides them, it is but to open drearier solitudes to the eye. In such a valley would stand a saw-mill, and huddled about it a few poor huts, while a friendless road, scarce discernible from the boat, wound up from the river through the valley, and led to wildernesses all the forlorner for the devastation of their forests. Now and then an island, rugged as the shores, broke the long reaches of the grim river with its massive rock and dark evergreen, and seemed in the distance to forbid escape from those dreary waters, over which no bird flew, and in which it was incredible any fish swam.

Mrs. Ellison, with her foot comfortably and not ungracefully supported on a stool, was in so little pain as to be looking from time to time at one of the guide-books which the colonel had lavished upon his party, and which she was disposed to hold to very strict account for any excesses of description.

"It says here that the water of the Saguenay is as black as ink. Do *you* think it is, Richard?"

W. D. Howells

"It looks so."

"Well, but if you took some up in your hand?"

"Perhaps it wouldn't be as black as the best Maynard and Noyes, but it would be black enough for all practical purposes."

"Maybe," suggested Kitty, "the guide-book means the kind that is light blue at first, but 'becomes a deep black on exposure to the air,' as the label says."

"What do you think, Mr. Arbuton?" asked Mrs. Ellison with unabated anxiety.

"Well, really, I don't know," said Mr. Arbuton, who thought it a very trivial kind of talk, "I can't say, indeed. I haven't taken any of it up in my hand."

"That's true," said Mrs. Ellison gravely, with an accent of reproval for the others who had not thought of so simple a solution of the problem, "very true."

The colonel looked into her face with an air of well-feigned alarm. "You don't think the sprain has gone to your head, Fanny?" he asked, and walked away, leaving Mr. Arbuton to the ladies. Mrs. Ellison did not care for this or any other gibe, if she but served her own purposes; and now, having made everybody laugh and given the conversation a lively turn, she was as perfectly content as if she had not been herself an offering to the cause of cheerfulness. She was, indeed, equal to any sacrifice in the enterprise she had undertaken, and would not only have given Kitty all her worldly goods, but would have quite effaced herself to further her own designs upon Mr. Arbuton. She turned again to her guide-book, and left the young people to continue the talk in unbroken gayety. They at once became serious, as most people do after a hearty laugh, which, if you think, seems always to have something strange and sad in it. But besides, Kitty was oppressed by the coldness that seemed perpetually to hover in Mr. Arbuton's atmosphere, while she was interested by his fastidious good looks and his blameless manners and his air of a world different from any she had hitherto known. He was one of those men whose perfection makes you feel guilty of misdemeanor whenever they meet you, and whose greeting turns your honest good-day coarse and common; even Kitty's fearless ignorance and more than Western disregard of dignities were not proof against him. She had found it easy to talk with Mrs. March as she did with her cousin at home: she liked to be frank and gay in her parley, to jest and to laugh and to make harmless fun, and to sentimentalize in a half-earnest way; she liked to be with Mr. Arbuton, but now she did not see how she could take her natural tone with him. She wondered at her daring lightness at the breakfast-table; she waited for him to say something, and he said, with a glance at the gray heaven that always overhangs the Saguenay, that it was beginning to rain, and unfurled the slender silk umbrella which harmonized so perfectly with the London effect of his dress, and held it over her. Mrs. Ellison sat within the shelter of the projecting roof, and diligently perused her book with her eyes, and listened to their talk.

"The great drawback to this sort of thing in America," continued Mr. Arbuton, "is that there is no human interest about the scenery, fine as it is."

"Why, I don't know," said Kitty, "there was that little settlement round the saw-mill. Can't you imagine any human interest in the lives of the people there? It seems to me that one might make almost anything out of them. Suppose, for example, that the owner of that mill was a disappointed man who had come here to bury the wreck of his life in—sawdust?"

"O, yes! That sort of thing; certainly. But I didn't mean that, I meant something historical. There is no past, no atmosphere, no traditions, you know."

"O, but the Saguenay *has* a tradition," said Kitty. "You know that a party of the first explorers left their comrades at

Tadoussac, and came up the Saguenay three hundred years ago, and never were seen or heard of again. I think it's so in keeping with the looks of the river. The Saguenay would never tell a secret."

"Um!" uttered Mr. Arbuton, as if he were not quite sure that it was the Saguenay's place to have a legend of this sort, and disposed to snub the legend because the Saguenay had it. After a little silence, he began to speak of famous rivers abroad.

"I suppose," Kitty said, "the Rhine has traditions enough, hasn't it?"

"Yes," he answered, "but I think the Rhine rather overdoes it. You can't help feeling, you know, that it's somewhat melodramatic and—common. Have you ever seen the Rhine?"

"O, no! This is almost the first I've seen of anything. Perhaps," she added, demurely, yet with a tremor at finding herself about to make light of Mr. Arbuton, "if I had had too much of tradition on the Rhine I should want more of it on the Saguenay."

"Why, you must allow there's a golden mean in everything, Miss Ellison," said her companion with a lenient laugh, not feeling it disagreeable to be made light of by her.

"Yes; and I'm afraid we're going to find Cape Trinity and Cape Eternity altogether too big when we come to them. Don't you think eighteen hundred feet excessively high for a feature of river scenery?"

Mr. Arbuton really did have an objection to the exaggerations of nature on this continent, and secretly thought them in bad taste, but he had never formulated his feeling. He was not sure but it was ridiculous, now that it was suggested, and yet the possibility was too novel to be entertained without suspicion.

However, when after a while the rumor of their approach to

the great objects of the Saguenay journey had spread among the passengers, and they began to assemble at points favorable for the enjoyment of the spectacle, he was glad to have secured the place he held with Miss Ellison, and a sympathetic thrill of excitement passed through his loath superiority. The rain ceased as they drew nearer, and the gray clouds that had hung so low upon the hills sullenly lifted from them and let their growing height he seen. The captain bade his sight-seers look at the vast Roman profile that showed itself upon the rock, and then he pointed out the wonderful Gothic arch, the reputed doorway of an unexplored cavern, under which an upright shaft of stone had stood for ages statue-like, till not many winters ago the frost heaved it from its base, and it plunged headlong down through the ice into the unfathomed depths below. The unvarying gloom of the pines was lit now by the pensive glimmer of birch-trees, and this gray tone gave an indescribable sentiment of pathos and of age to the scenery. Suddenly the boat rounded the corner of the three steps, each five hundred feet high, in which Cape Eternity climbs from the river, and crept in under the naked side of the awful cliff. It is sheer rock, springing from the black water, and stretching upward with a weary, effort-like aspect, in long impulses of stone marked by deep seams from space to space, till, fifteen hundred feet in air, its vast brow beetles forward, and frowns with a scattering fringe of pines. There are stains of weather and of oozing springs upon the front of the cliff, but it is height alone that seems to seize the eye, and one remembers afterwards these details, which are indeed so few as not properly to enter into the effect. The rock fully justifies its attributive height to the eye, which follows the upward rush of the mighty acclivity, steep after steep, till it wins the cloud-capt summit, when the measureless mass seems to swing and sway overhead, and the nerves tremble with the same terror that besets him who looks downward from the verge of a lofty precipice. It is wholly grim and stern; no touch of beauty relieves the austere majesty of that presence. At the foot of Cape Eternity the water is of unknown depth, and it spreads, a black expanse, in the rounding hollow of shores of unimaginable wildness and desolation, and issues again in its river's course around the base of Cape Trinity. This is yet loftier than the sister cliff, but it slopes gently backward from the stream, and from foot to crest it is heavily clothed with a forest of pines. The woods that hitherto have shagged the hills with a stunted and meagre growth, showing long stretches scarred by fire, now assume a stately size, and assemble themselves compactly upon the side of the mountain, setting their serried stems one rank above another, till the summit is crowned with the mass of their dark green plumes, dense and soft and beautiful; so that the spirit perturbed by the spectacle of the other cliff is calmed and assuaged by the serene grandeur of this.

There have been, to be sure, some human agencies at work even under the shadow of Cape Eternity to restore the spirit to self-possession, and perhaps none turns from it wholly dismayed. Kitty, at any rate, took heart from some works of art which the cliff wall displayed near the water's edge. One of these was a lively fresco portrait of Lieutenant-General Sherman, with the insignia of his rank, and the other was an even more striking effigy of General O'Neil, of the Armies of the Irish Republic, wearing a threatening aspect, and designed in a bold conceit of his presence there as conqueror of Canada in the year 1875. Mr. Arbuton was inclined to resent these intrusions upon the sublimity of nature, and he could not conceive, without disadvantage to them, how Miss Ellison and the colonel should accept them so cheerfully as part of the pleasure of the whole. As he listened blankly to their exchange of jests he found himself awfully beset by a temptation which one of the boat's crew placed before the passengers. This was a bucket full of pebbles of inviting size; and the man said, "Now, see which can hit the cliff. It's farther than any of you can throw, though it looks so near."

The passengers cast themselves upon the store of missiles, Colonel Ellison most actively among them. None struck the cliff, and suddenly Mr. Arbuton felt a blind, stupid, irresistible longing to try his chance. The spirit of his college days, of his boating and ball-playing youth, came upon him. He picked up a pebble, while Kitty opened her eyes in a stare of dumb surprise. Then he wheeled and threw it, and as it struck against the cliff with a shock that seemed to have broken all the windows on the Back Bay, he exulted in a sense of freedom the havoc caused him. It was as if for an instant he had rent away the ties of custom, thrown off the bonds of social allegiance, broken down and trampled upon the conventions which his whole life long he had held so dear and respectable. In that moment of frenzy he feared himself capable of shaking hands with the shabby Englishman in the Glengarry cap, or of asking the whole admiring company of passengers down to the bar. A cry of applause had broken from them at his achievement, and he had for the first time tasted the sweets of popular favor. Of course a revulsion must come, and it must be of a corresponding violence; and the next moment Mr. Arbuton hated them all, and most of all Colonel Ellison, who had been loudest in his praise. Him he thought for that moment everything that was aggressively and intrusively vulgar. But he could not utter these friendly impressions, nor is it so easy to withdraw from any concession, and he found it impossible to repair his broken defences. Destiny had been against him from the beginning, and now why should he not strike hands with it for the brief half-day that he was to continue in these people's society? In the morning he would part from them forever, and in the mean time why should he not try to please and be pleased? There might, to be sure, have been many reasons why he should not do this; but however the balance stood he now yielded himself passively to his fate. He was polite to Mrs. Ellison, he was attentive to Kitty, and as far as he could he entered into the fantastic spirit of her talk with the colonel. He was not a dull man; he had quite an apt wit of his own, and a neat way of saying things; but humor always seemed to him something not perfectly well bred; of course he helped to praise it in some old-established diner-out, or some woman of good fashion, whose *mots* it was customary to repeat, and he even tolerated it in books; but he was at a loss with these people, who looked at life in so bizarre a temper, yet without airiness or pretension, nay, with a whimsical readiness to acknowledge kindred in every droll or laughable thing.

The boat stopped at Tadoussac on her return, and among the spectators who came down to the landing was a certain very pretty, conscious-looking, silly, bridal-faced young woman,— imaginably the belle of the season at that forlorn watering-place,—who before coming on board stood awhile attended by a following of those elderly imperial and colonial British who heavily flutter round the fair at such resorts. She had an air of utterly satisfied vanity, in which there was no harm in the world, and when she saw that she had fixed the eyes of the shoreward-gazing passengers, it appeared as if she fell into a happy trepidation too blissful to be passively borne; she moistened her pretty red lips with her tongue, she twitched her mantle, she settled the bow at her lovely throat, she bridled and tossed her graceful head.

"What should you do next, Kitty?" asked the colonel, who had been sympathetically intent upon all this.

"O, I think I should pat my foot," answered Kitty; and in fact the charming simpleton on shore, having perfected her attitude, was tapping the ground nervously with the toe of her adorable slipper.

After the boat started, a Canadian lady of ripe age, yet of a vivacity not to be reconciled with the notion of the married state, capered briskly about among her somewhat stolid and indifferent friends, saying, "They're going to fire it as soon as we round the point"; and presently a dull boom, as of a small piece of ordnance discharged in the neighborhood of the hotel, struck through the gathering fog, and this elderly sylph clapped her hands and exulted: "They've fired it, they've fired it! and now the captain will blow the whistle in answer." But the captain did nothing of the kind, and the lady, after some more girlish effervescence, upbraided him for an old owl and an old muff, and so sank into such a flat and spiritless calm that she was sorrowful to see.

"Too bad, Mr. Arbuton, isn't it?" said the colonel; and Mr. Arbuton listened in vague doubt while Kitty built up with her cousin a touching romance for the poor lady, supposed to have spent the one brilliant and successful summer of her life at Tadoussac, where her admirers had agreed to bemoan her loss in this explosion of gunpowder. They asked him if he did not wish the captain *had* whistled; and "Oh!" shuddered Kitty, "doesn't it all make you feel just as if you had been doing it yourself?"—a question which he hardly knew how to answer, never having, to his knowledge, done a ridiculous thing in his life, much less been guilty of such behavior as that of the disappointed lady.

At Cacouna, where the boat stopped to take on the horses and carriages of some home-returning sojourners, the pier was a labyrinth of equipages of many sorts and sizes, and a herd of bright-hooded, gayly blanketed horses gave variety to the human crowd that soaked and steamed in the fine, slowly falling rain. A draught-horse was every three minutes driven into their midst with tedious iteration as he slowly drew baskets of coal up from the sloop unloading at the wharf, and each time they closed solidly upon his retreat as if they never expected to see that horse again while the world stood. They were idle ladies and gentlemen under umbrellas, Indians and habitans taking the rain stolidly erect or with shrugged shoulders, and two or three clergymen of the curate type, who might have stepped as they were out of any dull English novel. These were talking in low voices and putting their hands to their ears to catch the replies of the lady-passengers who hung upon the rail, and twaddled back as dryly as if there was no moisture in life. All the while the safety-valves hissed with the escaping steam, and the boat's crew silently toiled with the grooms of the different horses to get the equipages on board. With the carriages it was an affair of mere muscle, but the horses required to be managed with brain. No sooner had one of them placed his fore feet on the gangway plank than he protested by backing up over a mass of patient Canadians, carrying with him half a dozen grooms and deck-hands. Then his hood was drawn over his eyes, and he was blindly walked up and down the pier, and back to the gangway, which he knew as soon as he touched it. He pulled, he pranced, he

W. D. Howells

shied, he did all that a bad and stubborn horse can do, till at last a groom mounted his back, a clump of deck-hands tugged at his bridle, and other grooms, tenderly embracing him at different points, pushed, and he was thus conveyed on board with mingled affection and ignominy. None of the Canadians seemed amused by this; they regarded it with serious composure as a fitting decorum, and Mr. Arbuton had no comment to make upon it. But at the first embrace bestowed upon the horse by the grooms the colonel said absently, "Ah! long-lost brother," and Kitty laughed; and as the scruples of each brute were successively overcome, she helped to give some grotesque interpretation to the various scenes of the melodrama, while Mr. Arbuton stood beside her, and sheltered her with his umbrella; and a spice of malice in her heart told her that he viewed this drolling, and especially her part in it, with grave misgiving. That gave the zest of transgression to her excess, mixed with dismay; for the tricksy spirit in her was not a domineering spirit, but was easily abashed by the moods of others. She ought not to have laughed at Dick's speeches, she soon told herself, much less helped him on. She dreadfully feared that she had done something indecorous, and she was pensive and silent over it as she moved listlessly about after supper; and she sat at last thinking in a dreary sort of perplexity on what had passed during the day, which seemed a long one.

The shabby Englishman with his wife and sister were walking up and down the cabin. By and by they stopped, and sat down at the table facing Kitty; the elder woman, with a civil freedom, addressed her some commonplace, and the four were presently in lively talk; for Kitty had beamed upon the woman in return, having already longed to know something of them. The world was so fresh to her, that she could find delight in those poor singing or acting folk, though she had soon to own to herself that their talk was not very witty nor very wise, and that the best thing about them was their good-nature. The colonel sat at the end of the table with a newspaper; Mrs. Ellison had gone to bed; and Kitty was beginning to tire of her new acquaintance, and to wonder how she could get away from them, when she saw rescue in the eye of Mr. Arbuton as he came down to the cabin. She knew he was looking for her; she saw him check himself with a start of recognition; then he walked rapidly by the group, without glancing at them.

"Brrrr!" said the blond girl, drawing her blue knit shawl about her shoulders, "isn't it cold?" and she and her friends laughed.

"O dear!" thought Kitty, "I didn't suppose they were so rude. I'm afraid I must say good night," she added aloud, after a little, and stole away the most conscience-stricken creature on that boat. She heard those people laugh again after she left them.

IV

MR. ARBUTON'S INSPIRATION

The next morning, when Mr. Arbuton awoke, he found a clear light upon the world that he had left wrapped in fog at midnight. A heavy gale was blowing, and the wide river was running in seas that made the boat stagger in her course, and now and then struck her bows with a force that sent the spray from their seething tops into the faces of the people on the promenade. The sun, out of rifts of the breaking clouds, launched broad splendors across the villages and farms of the level landscape and the crests and hollows of the waves; and a certain joy of the air penetrated to the guarded consciousness of Mr. Arbuton. Involuntarily he looked about for the people he meant to have nothing more to do with, that he might appeal to the sympathies of one of them, at least, in his sense of such an admirable morning. But a great many passengers had come on board, during the night, at Murray Bay, where the brief season was ending, and their number hid the Ellisons from him. When he went to breakfast, he found some one had taken his seat near them, and they did not notice him as he passed by in search of another chair. Kitty and the colonel were at table alone, and they both wore preoccupied faces. After breakfast he sought them out and asked for Mrs. Ellison, who had shared in most of the excitements of the day before, helping herself about with a pretty limp, and who certainly had not, as her husband phrased it, kept any of the meals waiting.

"Why," said the colonel, "I'm afraid her ankle's worse this

morning, and that we'll have to lie by at Quebec for a few days, at any rate."

Mr. Arbuton heard this sad news with a cheerful aspect unaccountable in one who was concerned at Mrs. Ellison's misfortune. He smiled, when he ought to have looked pensive, and he laughed at the colonel's joke when the latter added, "Of course, this is a great hardship for my cousin, who hates Quebec, and wants to get home to Eriecreek as soon as possible."

Kitty promised to bear her trials with firmness, and Mr. Arbuton said, not very consequently, as she thought, "I had been planning to spend a few days in Quebec, myself, and I shall have the opportunity of inquiring about Mrs. Ellison's convalescence. In fact," he added, turning to the colonel, "I hope you'll let me be of service to you in getting to a hotel."

And when the boat landed, Mr. Arbuton actually busied himself in finding a carriage and putting the various Ellison wraps and bags into it. Then he helped to support Mrs. Ellison ashore, and to lift her to the best place. He raised his hat, and had good-morning on his tongue, when the astonished colonel called out, "Why, the deuce! You're going to ride up with us!"

Mr. Arbuton thought he had better get another carriage; he should incommode Mrs. Ellison; but Mrs. Ellison protested that he would not at all; and, to cut the matter short, he mounted to the colonel's side. It was another stroke of fate.

At the hotel they found a line of people reaching half-way down the outer steps from the inside of the office.

"Hallo! what's this?" asked the colonel of the last man in the queue.

"O, it's a little procession to the hotel register! We've been three quarters of an hour in passing a given point," said the man, who was plainly a fellow-citizen.

"And haven't got by yet," said the colonel, taking to the speaker. "Then the house is full?"

"Well, no; they haven't begun to throw them out of the window."

"His humor is degenerating, Dick," said Kitty; and "Hadn't you better go inside and inquire?" asked Mrs. Ellison. It was part of the Ellison travelling joke for her thus to prompt the colonel in his duty.

"I'm glad you mentioned it, Fanny. I was just going to drive off in despair." The colonel vanished within doors, and after long delay came out flushed, but not with triumph. "On the express condition that I have ladies with me, one an invalid, I am promised a room on the fifth floor some time during the day. They tell me the other hotel is crammed and it's no use to go there."

Mrs. Ellison was ready to weep, and for the first time since her accident she harbored some bitterness against Mr. Arbuton. They all sat silent, and the colonel on the sidewalk silently wiped his brow.

Mr. Arbuton, in the poverty of his invention, wondered if there was not some lodging-house where they could find shelter.

"Of course there is," cried Mrs. Ellison, beaming upon her hero, and calling Kitty's attention to his ingenuity by a pressure with her well foot. "Richard, we must look up a boarding-house."

"Do you know of any good boarding-houses?" asked the colonel of the driver, mechanically.

"Plenty," answered the man.

"Well, drive us to twenty or thirty first-class ones,"

commanded the colonel; and the search began.

The colonel first asked prices and looked at rooms, and if he pronounced any apartment unsuitable, Kitty was despatched by Mrs. Ellison to view it and refute him. As often as she confirmed him, Mrs. Ellison was sure that they were both too fastidious, and they never turned away from a door but they closed the gates of paradise upon that afflicted lady. She began to believe that they should find no place whatever, when at last they stopped before a portal so unboarding-house-like in all outward signs, that she maintained it was of no use to ring, and imparted so much of her distrust to the colonel that, after ringing, he prefaced his demand for rooms with an apology for supposing that there were rooms to let there. Then, after looking at them, he returned to the carriage and reported that the whole affair was perfect, and that he should look no farther. Mrs. Ellison replied that she never could trust his judgment, he was so careless. Kitty inspected the premises, and came back in a transport that alarmed the worst fears of Mrs. Ellison. She was sure that they had better look farther, she knew there were plenty of nicer places. Even if the rooms were nice and the situation pleasant, she was certain that there must be some drawbacks which they did not know of yet. Whereupon her husband lifted her from the carriage, and bore her, without reply or comment of any kind, into the house.

Throughout the search Mr. Arbuton had been making up his mind that he would part with his friends as soon as they found lodgings, give the day to Quebec, and take the evening train for Gorham, thus escaping the annoyances of a crowded hotel, and ending at once an acquaintance which he ought never to have let go so far. As long as the Ellisons were without shelter, he felt that it was due to himself not to abandon them. But even now that they were happily housed, had he done all that nobility obliged? He stood irresolute beside the carriage.

"Won't you come up and see where we live?" asked Kitty, hospitably.

"I shall be very glad," said Mr. Arbuton.

"My dear fellow," said the colonel, in the parlor, "I didn't engage a room for you. I supposed you'd rather take your chances at the hotel."

"O, I'm going away to-night."

"Why, that's a pity!"

"Yes, I've no fancy for a cot-bed in the hotel parlor. But I don't quite like to leave you here, after bringing this calamity upon you."

"O, don't mention that! I was the only one to blame. We shall get on splendidly here."

Mr. Arbuton suffered a vague disappointment. At the bottom of his heart was a formless hope that he might in some way be necessary to the Ellisons in their adversity; or if not that, then that something might entangle him further and compel his stay. But they seemed quite equal in themselves to the situation; they were in far more comfortable quarters than they could have hoped for, and plainly should want for nothing; Fortune put on a smiling face, and bade him go free of them. He fancied it a mocking smile, though, as he stood an instant silently weighing one thing against another. The colonel was patiently waiting his motion; Mrs. Ellison sat watching him from the sofa; Kitty moved about the room with averted face,—a pretty domestic presence, a household priestess ordering the temporary Penates. Mr. Arbuton opened his lips to say farewell, but a god spoke through them,—inconsequently, as the gods for the most part do, saying, "Besides, I suppose you've got all the rooms here."

"O, as to that I don't know," answered the colonel, not recognizing the language of inspiration, "let's ask." Kitty knocked a photograph-book off the table, and Mrs. Ellison said, "Why, Kitty!" But nothing more was spoken till the landlady came. She had another room, but doubted if it would answer. It was in the attic, and was a back room, though it had a pleasant outlook. Mr. Arbuton had no doubt that it would do very well for the day or two he was going to stay, and took it hastily, without going to look at it. He had his valise carried up at once, and then he went to the post-office to see if he had any letters, offering to ask also for Colonel Ellison.

Kitty stole off to explore the chamber given her at the rear of the house; that is to say, she opened the window looking out on what their hostess told her was the garden of the Ursuline Convent, and stood there in a mute transport. A black cross rose in the midst, and all about this wandered the paths and alleys of the garden, through clumps of lilac-bushes and among the spires of hollyhocks. The grounds were enclosed by high walls in part, and in part by the group of the convent edifices, built of gray stone, high gabled, and topped by dormer-windowed steep roofs of tin, which, under the high morning sun, lay an expanse of keenest splendor, while many a grateful shadow dappled the full-foliaged garden below. Two slim, tall poplars stood against the gable of the chapel, and shot their tops above its roof, and under a porch near them two nuns sat motionless in the sun, black-robed, with black veils falling over their shoulders, and their white faces lost in the white linen that draped them from breast to crown. Their hands lay quiet in their laps, and they seemed unconscious of the other nuns walking in the garden-paths with little children, their pupils, and answering their laughter from time to time with voices as simple and innocent as their own. Kitty looked down upon them all with a swelling heart. They were but figures in a beautiful picture of something old and poetical; but she loved them, and pitied them, and was most happy in them, the same as if they had been real. It could not be that they and she were in the same world: she must be dreaming over a book in Charley's room at Eriecreek. She shaded her eyes for a better look, when the noonday gun boomed from the citadel; the bell upon the chapel jangled harshly, and those strange maskers, those quaint black birds with white breasts and faces, flocked indoors. At the same time a small dog under her window howled dolorously at the jangling of the bell; and Kitty, with an impartial joy, turned from the pensive romance of the convent garden to the mild comedy of the scene to which his woeful note attracted her. When he had uttered his anguish, he relapsed into the quietest small French dog that ever was, and lay down near a large, tranquil cat, whom neither the bell nor he had been able to stir from her slumbers in the sun; a peasant-like old man kept on sawing wood, and a little child stood still amidst the larkspurs and marigolds of a tiny garden, while over the flower-pots on the low window-sill of the neighboring house to which it belonged, a young, motherly face gazed peacefully out. The great extent of the convent grounds had left this poor garden scarce breathing-space for its humble blooms; with the low paling fence that separated it from the adjoining house-yards it looked like a toy-garden or the background of a puppet-show, and in its way it was as quaintly unreal to the young girl as the nunnery itself.

When she saw it first, the city's walls and other warlike ostentations had taken her imagination with the historic grandeur of Quebec; but the fascination deepened now that she was admitted, as it were, to the religious heart and the domestic privacy of the famous old town. She was romantic, as most good young girls are; and she had the same pleasure in the strangeness of the things about her as she would have felt in the keeping of a charming story. To Fanny's "Well, Kitty, I suppose all this just suits you," when she had returned to the little parlor where the sufferer lay, she answered with a sigh of irrepressible content, "O yes! could anything be more beautiful?" and her enraptured eye dwelt upon the low ceilings, the deep, wide chimneys eloquent of the mighty fires with which they must roar in winter, the French windows with their curious and clumsy fastenings, and every little detail that made the place alien and precious.

Fanny broke into a laugh at the visionary absence in her face.

"Do you think the place is good enough for your hero and heroine?" asked she, slyly; for Kitty had one of those family reputes, so hard to survive, for childish attempts of her own in the world of fiction where so great part of her life had been passed; and Mrs. Ellison, who was as unliterary a soul as ever breathed, admired her with the heartiness which unimaginative people often feel for their idealizing friends, and believed that she was always deep in the mysteries of some plot.

"O, I don't know," Kitty answered with a little color, "about heroes and heroines; but, I'd like to live here, myself. Yes," she continued, rather to herself than to her listener, "I do believe this is what I was made for. I've always wanted to live amongst old things, in a stone house with dormer-windows. Why, there isn't a single dormer-window in Eriecreek, nor even a brick house, let alone a stone one. O yes, indeed! I was meant for an old country."

"Well, then, Kitty, I don't see what you're to do but to marry East and live East; or else find a rich husband, and get him to take you to Europe to live."

"Yes; or get him to come and live in Quebec. That's all I'd ask, and he needn't be a very rich man, for that."

"Why, you poor child, what sort of husband could you get to settle down in *this* dead old place?"

"O, I suppose some kind of artist or literary man."

This was not Mrs. Ellison's notion of the kind of husband who was to realize for Kitty her fancy for life in an old country; but she was content to let the matter rest for the present, and, in a serene thankfulness to the power that had brought two marriageable young creatures together beneath the same roof, and under her own observance, she composed herself among the sofa-cushions, from which she meant to conduct the campaign against Mr. Arbuton with relentless vigor.

"Well," she said, "it won't be fair if you are not happy in this world, Kitty, you ask so little of it"; while Kitty turned to the window overlooking the street, and lost herself in the drama of the passing figures below. They were new, and yet oddly familiar, for she had long known them in the realm of romance. The peasant-women who went by, in hats of felt or straw, some on foot with baskets, and some in their light market-carts, were all, in their wrinkled and crooked age or their fresh-faced, strong-limbed youth, her friends since childhood in many a tale of France or Germany; and the black-robed priests, who mixed with the passers on the narrow wooden sidewalk, and now and then courteously gave way, or lifted their wide-rimmed hats in a grave, smiling salutation, were more recent acquaintances, but not less intimate. They were out of old romances about Italy and Spain, in which she was very learned; and this butcher's boy, tilting along through the crowd with a half-staggering run, was from any one of Dickens's stories, and she divined that the four-armed wooden trough on his shoulder was the butcher's tray, which figures in every novelist's description of a London street-crowd. There were many other types, as French mothers of families with market-baskets on their arms; very pretty French school-girls with books under their arms; wild-looking country boys with red raspberries in birch-bark measures; and quiet gliding nuns with white hoods and downcast faces: each of whom she unerringly relegated to an appropriate corner of her world of unreality. A young, mild-faced, spectacled Anglican curate she did not give a moment's pause, but rushed him instantly through the whole series of Anthony Trollope's novels, which dull books, I am sorry to say, she had read, and liked, every one; and then she began to find various people astray out of Thackeray. The trig corporal, with the little visorless cap worn so jauntily, the light stick carried in one hand, and the broad-sealed official document in the other, had also, in his breast-pocket, one of those brief, infrequent missives which Lieutenant Osborne used to send to poor Amelia; a tall, awkward officer did duty for Major Dobbin; and when a very pretty lady driving a pony carriage, with a footman in livery on the little perch behind her, drew rein beside the pavement, and a handsome young captain in a splendid uniform saluted her and began talking with her in a languid, affected way, it was

Osborne recreant to the thought of his betrothed, one of whose tender letters he kept twirling in his fingers while he talked.

Most of the people whom she saw passing had letters or papers, and, in fact, they were coming from the post-office, where the noonday mails had just been opened. So she went on turning substance into shadow,—unless, indeed, flesh and blood is the illusion,—and, as I am bound to own, catching at very slight pretexts in many cases for the exercise of her sorcery, when her eye fell upon a gentleman at a little distance. At the same moment he raised his eyes from a letter at which he had been glancing, and ran them along the row of houses opposite, till they rested on the window at which she stood. Then he smiled and lifted his hat, and, with a start, she recognized Mr. Arbuton, while a certain chill struck to her heart through the tumult she felt there. Till he saw her there had been such a cold reserve and hauteur in his bearing, that the trepidation which she had felt about him at times, the day before, and which had worn quite away under the events of the morning, was renewed again, and the aspect, in which he had been so strange that she did not know him, seemed the only one that he had ever worn. This effect lasted till Mr. Arbuton could find his way to her, and place in her eager hand a letter from the girls and Dr. Ellison. She forgot it then, and vanished till she read her letter.

W. D. Howells

V

MR. ARBUTON MAKES HIMSELF AGREEABLE

The first care of Colonel Ellison had been to call a doctor, and to know the worst about the sprained ankle, upon which his plans had fallen lame; and the worst was that it was not a bad sprain, but Mrs. Ellison, having been careless of it the day before, had aggravated the hurt, and she must now have that perfect rest, which physicians prescribe so recklessly of other interests and duties, for a week at least, and possibly two or three.

The colonel was still too much a soldier to be impatient at the doctor's order, but he was of far too active a temper to be quiet under it. He therefore proposed to himself nothing less than the capture of Quebec in an historical sense, and even before dinner he began to prepare for the campaign. He sallied forth, and descended upon the bookstores wherever he found them lurking, in whatsoever recess of the Upper or Lower Town, and returned home laden with guide-books to Quebec, and monographs upon episodes of local history, such as are produced in great quantity by the semi-clerical literary taste of out-of-the-way Catholic capitals. The colonel (who had gone actively into business, after leaving the army, at the close of the war) had always a newspaper somewhere about him, but he was not a reader of many books. Of the volumes in the doctor's library, he had never in former days willingly opened any but the plays of Shakespeare, and Don Quixote, long passages of which he knew by heart. He had sometimes attempted other books, but for the most of Kitty's favorite authors he professed as frank a contempt as for the Mound-Builders themselves. He had read one book of travel, namely, The Innocents Abroad, which he held to be so good a book that he need never read anything else about the countries of which it treated. When he brought in this extraordinary collection of pamphlets, both Kitty and Fanny knew what to expect; for the colonel was as ready to receive literature at second-hand as to avoid its original sources. He had in this way picked up a great deal of useful knowledge, and he was famous for clipping from newspapers scraps of instructive fact, all of which he relentlessly remembered. He had already a fair outline of the local history in his mind, and this had been deepened and freshened by Dr. Ellison's recent talk of his historical studies. Moreover, he had secured in the course of the present journey, from his wife's and cousin's reading of divers guide-books, a new store of names and dates, which he desired to attach to the proper localities with their help.

"Light reading for leisure hours, Fanny," said Kitty, looking askance at the colonel's literature as she sat down near her cousin after dinner.

"Yes; and you start fair, ladies. Start with Jacques Cartier, ancient mariner of Dieppe, in the year 1535. No favoritism in this investigation; no bringing forward of Champlain or Montcalm prematurely; no running off on subsequent conquests or other side-issues. Stick to the discovery, and the names of Jacques Cartier and Donnacona. Come, do something for an honest living."

"Who was Donnacona?" demanded Mrs. Ellison, with indifference.

"That is just what these fascinating little volumes will tell us. Kitty, read something to your suffering cousins about Donnacona,—he sounds uncommonly like an Irishman," answered the colonel, establishing himself in an easy-chair; and Kitty picked up a small sketch of the history of Quebec, and, opening it, fell into the trance which came upon her at the touch of a book, and read on for some pages to herself.

"Well, upon my word," said the colonel, "I might as well be reading about Donnacona myself, for any comfort I get."

"O Dick, I forgot. I was just looking. Now I'm really going to commence."

"No, not yet," cried Mrs. Ellison, rising on her elbow. "Where is Mr. Arbuton?"

"What has he to do with Donnacona, my dear?"

"Everything. You know he's stayed on our account, and I never heard of anything so impolite, so inhospitable, as offering to read without him. Go and call him, Richard, do."

"O, no," pleaded Kitty, "he won't care about it. Don't call him, Dick."

"Why, Kitty, I'm surprised at you! When you read so beautifully! Yon needn't be ashamed, I'm sure."

"I'm not ashamed; but, at the same time, I don't want to read to him."

"Well, call him any way, colonel. He's in his room."

"If you do," said Kitty, with superfluous dignity, "I must go away."

"Very well, Kitty, just as you please. Only I want Richard to witness that I'm not to blame if Mr. Arbuton thinks us unfeeling or neglectful."

"O, if he doesn't say what he thinks, it'll make no difference."

"It seems to me that this is a good deal of fuss to make about one human being, a mere passing man and brother of a day, isn't it?" said the colonel. "Go on with Donnacona, do."

There came a knock at the door. Kitty leaped nervously to her feet, and fled out of the room. But it was only the little French serving-maid upon some errand which she quickly despatched.

"Well, *now* what do you think?" asked Mrs. Ellison.

"Why, I think you've a surprising knowledge of French for one who studied it at school. Do you suppose she understood you?"

"O, nonsense! You know I mean Kitty and her very queer behavior. Richard, if you moon at me in that stupid way," she continued, "I shall certainly end in an insane asylum. Can't you see what's under your very nose?"

"Yes, I can, Fanny," answered the colonel, "if anything's there. But I give you my word, I don't know any more than millions yet unborn what you're driving at." The colonel took up the book which Kitty had thrown down, and went to his room to try to read up Donnacona for himself, while his wife penitently turned to a pamphlet in French, which he had bought with the others. "After all," she thought, "men will be men"; and seemed not to find the fact wholly wanting in consolation.

A few minutes after there was a murmur of voices in the entry without, at a window looking upon the convent garden, where it happened to Mr. Arbuton, descending from his attic chamber, to find Kitty standing, a pretty shape against the reflected light of the convent roofs, and amidst a little greenery of house-plants, tall geraniums, an overarching ivy, some delicate roses. She had paused there, on her way from Fanny's to her own room, and was looking into the garden, where a pair of silent nuns were pacing up and down the paths, turning now their backs with the heavy sable coiffure sweeping their black robes, and now their still, mask-like faces, set in that stiff framework of white linen. Sometimes they came so near that she could distinguish their features, and imagine an expression that she should know if she saw them again; and while she stood self-forgetfully feigning a character for each of them, Mr. Arbuton spoke to her and took his place at her side.

"We're remarkably favored in having this bit of opera under our windows, Miss Ellison," he said, and smiled as Kitty answered, "O, is it really like an opera? I never saw one, but I could imagine it must be beautiful," and they both looked on in silence a moment, while the nuns moved, shadow-like, out of the garden, and left it empty.

Then Mr. Arbuton said something to which Kitty answered simply, "I'll see if my cousin doesn't want me," and presently stood beside Mrs. Ellison's sofa, a little conscious in color. "Fanny, Mr. Arbuton has asked me to go and see the cathedral with him. Do you think it would be right?"

Mrs. Ellison's triumphant heart rose to her lips. "Why, you dear, particular, innocent little goose," she cried, flinging her arms about Kitty, and kissing her till the young girl blushed again; "of course it would! Go! You mustn't stay mewed up in here. *I* sha'n't be able to go about with you; and if I can judge by the colonel's *breathing*, as he calls it, from the room in there, *he* won't, at present. But the idea of *your* having a question of propriety!" And indeed it was the first time Kitty had ever had such a thing, and the remembrance of it put a kind of constraint upon her, as she strolled demurely beside Mr. Arbuton towards the cathedral.

"You must be guide," said he, "for this is my first day in Quebec, you know, and you are an old inhabitant in comparison."

"I'll show the way," she answered, "if you'll interpret the sights. I think I must be stranger to them than you, in spite of my long residence. Sometimes I'm afraid that I *do* only fancy I enjoy these things, as Mrs. March said, for I've no European experiences to contrast them with. I know that it *seems* very delightful, though, and quite like what I should expect in Europe."

"You'd expect very little of Europe, then, in most things; though there's no disputing that it's a very pretty illusion of the Old World."

A few steps had brought them into the market-square in front of the cathedral, where a little belated traffic still lingered in the few old peasant-women hovering over baskets of such fruits and vegetables as had long been out of season in the States, and the housekeepers and serving-maids cheapening these wares. A sentry moved mechanically up and down before the high portal of the Jesuit Barracks, over the arch of which were still the letters I. H. S. carved long ago upon the keystone; and the ancient edifice itself, with its yellow stucco front and its grated windows, had every right to be a monastery turned barracks in France or Italy. A row of quaint stone houses—inns and shops—formed the upper side of the Square; while the modern buildings of the Rue Fabrique on the lower side might serve very well for that show of improvement which deepens the sentiment of the neighboring antiquity and decay in Latin towns. As for the cathedral, which faced the convent from across the Square, it was as cold and torpid a bit of Renaissance as could be found in Rome itself. A red-coated soldier or two passed through the Square; three or four neat little French policemen lounged about in blue uniforms and flaring havelocks; some walnut-faced, blue-eyed old citizens and peasants sat upon the thresholds of the row of old houses, and gazed dreamily through the smoke of their pipes at the slight stir and glitter of shopping about the fine stores of the Rue Fabrique. An air of serene disoccupation pervaded the place, with which the occasional riot of the drivers of the long row of calashes and carriages in front of the cathedral did not discord. Whenever a stray American wandered into the Square, there was a wild flight of these drivers towards him, and his person was lost to sight amidst their pantomime. They did not try to underbid each other, and they were perfectly good-humored; as soon as he had made his choice, the rejected multitude returned to their places on the curbstone, pursuing the successful aspirant with inscrutable jokes as he drove off, while the horses went on munching the contents of their leathern head-bags, and tossing them into the air to shake down the lurking grains of corn.

"It *is* like Europe; your friends were right," said Mr. Arbuton as they escaped into the cathedral from one of these friendly onsets. "It's quite the atmosphere of foreign travel, and you ought to be able to realize the feelings of a tourist."

A priest was saying mass at one of the side-altars, assisted by acolytes in their every-day clothes; and outside of the railing a market-woman, with a basket of choke-cherries, knelt among a few other poor people. Presently a young English couple came in, he with a dashing India scarf about his hat, and she very stylishly dressed, who also made their genuflections with the rest, and then sat down and dropped their heads in prayer.

"This is like enough Europe, too," murmured Mr. Arbuton. "It's very good North Italy; or South, for the matter of that."

"O, is it?" answered Kitty, joyously. "I thought it must be!" And she added, in that trustful way of hers: "It's all very familiar; but then it seems to me on this journey that I've seen a great many things that I know I've only read of before"; and so followed Mr. Arbuton in his tour of the pictures.

She was as ignorant of art as any Roman or Florentine girl whose life has been passed in the midst of it; and she believed these mighty fine pictures, and was puzzled by Mr. Arbuton's behavior towards them, who was too little imaginative or too conscientious to make merit for them out of the things they suggested. He treated the poor altar-pieces of the Quebec cathedral with the same harsh indifference he would have shown to the second-rate paintings of a European gallery; doubted the Vandyck, and cared nothing for the Conception, "in the style of Le Brun," over the high-altar, though it had the historical interest of having survived that bombardment of

1759 which destroyed the church.

Kitty innocently singled out the worst picture in the place as
her favorite, and then was piqued, and presently frightened, at
his cold reluctance about it. He made her feel that it was very
bad, and that she shared its inferiority, though he said nothing
to that effect. She learned the shame of not being a connoisseur in a connoisseur's company, and she perceived more
painfully than ever before that a Bostonian, who had been
much in Europe, might be very uncomfortable to the simple,
unravelled American. Yet, she reminded herself, the Marches
had been in Europe, and they were Bostonians also; and they
did not go about putting everything under foot; they seemed
to care for everything they saw, and to have a friendly jest, if
not praises, for it. She liked that; she would have been well
enough pleased to have Mr. Arbuton laugh outright at her
picture, and she could have joined him in it. But the look,
however flattered into an air of polite question at last, which
he had bent upon her, seemed to outlaw her and condemn her
taste in everything. As they passed out of the cathedral, she
would rather have gone home than continued the walk as he
begged her, if she were not tired, to do; but this would have
been flight, and she was not a coward. So they sauntered down
the Rue Fabrique, and turned into Palace Street. As they went
by the door of Hotel Musty, her pleasant friends came again
into her mind, and she said, "This is where we stayed last
week, with Mr. and Mrs. March."

"Those Boston people?"

"Yes."

"Do you know where they live in Boston?"

"Why, we have their address; but I can't think of it. I believe
somewhere in the southern part of the city—"

"The South End?"

"O yes, that's it. Have you ever heard of them?"

"No."

"I thought perhaps you might have known Mr. March. He's in the insurance business—"

"O no! No, I don't know him," said Mr. Arbuton, eagerly. Kitty wondered if there could be anything wrong with the business repute of Mr. March, but dismissed the thought as unworthy; and having perceived that her friends were snubbed, she said bravely, that they were the most delightful people she had ever seen, and she was sorry that they were not still in Quebec. He shared her regret tacitly, if at all, and they walked in silence to the gate, whence they strolled down the winding street outside the wall into the Lower Town. But it was not a pleasant ramble for Kitty: she was in a dim dread of hitherto unseen and unimagined trespasses against good taste, not only in pictures and people, but in all life, which, from having been a very smiling prospect when she set out with Mr. Arbuton, had suddenly become a narrow pathway, in which one must pick one's way with more regard to each step than any general end. All this was as obscure and uncertain as the intimations which had produced it, and which, in words, had really amounted to nothing. But she felt more and more that in her companion there was something wholly alien to the influences which had shaped her; and though she could not know how much, she was sure of enough to make her dreary in his presence.

They wandered through the quaintness and noiseless bustle of the Lower Town thoroughfares, and came by and by to that old church, the oldest in Quebec, which was built near two hundred years ago, in fulfilment of a vow made at the repulse of Sir William Phipps's attack upon the city, and further famed for the prophecy of a nun, that this church should be ruined by the fire in which a successful attempt of the English was yet to involve the Lower Town. A painting, which represented the vision of the nun, perished in the conflagration which verified it, in 1759; but the walls of the ancient structure remain to witness this singular piece of history, which Kitty now glanced at furtively in one of the colonel's guide-books; since her ill-fortune with the picture in the cathedral, she had not openly cared for anything.

At one side of the church there was a booth for the sale of crockery and tin ware; and there was an every-day cheerfulness of small business in the shops and tented stands about the square on which the church faced, and through which there was continual passing of heavy burdens from the port, swift calashes, and slow, country-paced market-carts.

Mr. Arbuton made no motion to enter the church, and Kitty would not hint the curiosity she felt to see the interior; and while they lingered a moment, the door opened, and a peasant came out with a little coffin in his arms. His eyes were dim and his face wet with weeping, and he bore the little coffin tenderly, as if his caress might reach the dead child within. Behind him she came who must be the mother, her face deeply hidden in her veil. Beside the pavement waited a shabby calash, with a driver half asleep on his perch; and the man, still clasping his precious burden, clambered into the vehicle, and laid it upon his knees, while the woman groped, through her tears and veil, for the step. Kitty and her companion had moved reverently aside; but now Mr. Arbuton came forward, and helped the woman to her place. She gave him a hoarse, sad "*Merci!*" and spread a fold of her shawl fondly over the end of the little coffin; the drowsy driver whipped up his beast, and the calash jolted away.

Kitty cast a grateful glance upon Mr. Arbuton, as they now entered the church, by a common impulse. On their way towards the high-altar they passed the rude black bier, with the tallow candles yet smoking in their black wooden candlesticks. A few worshippers were dropped here and there in the vacant seats, and at a principal side-altar knelt a poor woman praying before a wooden effigy of the dead Christ that lay in a glass case under the altar. The image was of life-size, and was

W. D. Howells

painted to represent life, or rather death, with false hair and beard, and with the muslin drapery managed to expose the stigmata: it was stretched upon a bed strewn with artificial flowers; and it was dreadful. But the poor soul at her devotions there prayed to it in an ecstasy of supplication, flinging her arms asunder with imploring gesture, clasping her hands and bowing her head upon them, while her person swayed from side to side in the abandon of her prayer. Who could she be, and what was her mighty need of blessing or forgiveness? As her wont was, Kitty threw her own soul into the imagined case of the suppliant, the tragedy of her desire or sorrow. Yet, like all who suffer sympathetically, she was not without consolations unknown to the principal; and the waning afternoon, as it lit up the conventional ugliness of the old church, and the paraphernalia of its worship, relieved her emotional self-abandon with a remote sense of content, so that it may have been a jealousy for the integrity of her own revery, as well as a feeling for the poor woman, that made her tremble lest Mr. Arbuton should in some way disparage the spectacle. I suppose that her interest in it was more an aesthetic than a spiritual one; it embodied to her sight many a scene of penitence that had played before her fancy, and I do not know but she would have been willing to have the suppliant guilty of some dreadful misdeed, rather than eating meat last Friday, which was probably her sin. However it was, the ancient crone before that ghastly idol was precious to her, and it seemed too great a favor, when at last the suppliant wiped her eyes, rose trembling from her knees, and approaching Kitty, stretched towards her a shaking palm for charity.

It was a touch that transfigured all, and gave even Mr. Arbuton's neutrality a light of ideal character. He bestowed the alms craved of him in turn, he did not repulse the beldame's blessing; and Kitty, who was already moved by his kindness to that poor mourner at the door, forgot that the earlier part of their walk had been so miserable, and climbed back to the Upper Town through the Prescott Gate in greater gayety than she had yet known that day in his company. I think he had not done much to make her cheerful; but it is one of the advantages of a temperament like his, that very little is expected of it, and that it can more easily than any other make the human heart glad; at the least softening in it, the soul frolics with a craven lightsomeness. For this reason Kitty was able to enjoy with novel satisfaction the picturesqueness of Mountain Street, and they both admired the huge shoulder of rock near the gate, with its poplars atop, and the battery at the brink, with the muzzles of the guns thrust forward against the sky. She could not move him to her pleasure in the grotesqueness of the circus-bills plastered half-way up the rock; but he tolerated the levity with which she commented on them, and her light sallies upon passing things, and he said nothing to prevent her reaching home in serene satisfaction.

"Well, Kitty," said the tenant of the sofa, as Kitty and the colonel drew up to the table on which the tea was laid at the sofa-side, "you've had a nice walk, haven't you?"

"O yes, very nice. That is, the first part of it wasn't very nice; but after a while we reached an old church in the Lower Town,—which was very interesting,—and then we appeared to cheer up and take a new start."

"Well," asked the colonel, "what did you find so interesting at that old church?"

"Why, there was a baby's funeral; and an old woman, perfectly crushed by some trouble or other, praying before an altar, and—"

"It seems to take very little to cheer you up," said the colonel. "All you ask of your fellow-beings is a heart-breaking bereavement and a religious agony, and you are lively at once. *Some* people might require human sacrifices, but you don't."

Kitty looked at her cousin a moment with vague amaze. The grossness of the absurdity flashed upon her, and she felt as if another touch must bring the tears. She said nothing; but Mrs. Ellison, who saw only that she was cut off from her heart's desire of gossip, came to the rescue.

"Don't answer a word, Kitty, not a single word; I never heard anything more insulting from one cousin to another; and I should say it, if I was brought into a court of justice."

A sudden burst of laughter from Kitty, who hid her conscious face in her hands, interrupted Mrs. Ellison's defence.

"Well," said Mrs. Ellison, piqued at her desertion, "I hope you understand yourselves. *I* don't." This was Mrs. Ellison's attitude towards her husband's whole family, who on their part never had been able to account for the colonel's choice except as a joke, and sometimes questioned if he had not perhaps carried the joke too far; though they loved her too, for a kind of passionate generosity and sublime, inconsequent unselfishness about her.

"What I want to know, *now*," said the colonel, as soon as Kitty would let him, "and I'll try to put it as politely as I can, is simply this: what made the first part of your walk so disagreeable? You didn't see a wedding-party, or a child rescued from a horrible death, or a man saved from drowning, or anything of that kind, did you?"

But the colonel would have done better not to say anything. His wife was made peevish by his persistence, and the loss of the harmless pleasure upon which she had counted in the history of Kitty's walk with Mr. Arbuton. Kitty herself would not laugh again; in fact she grew serious and thoughtful, and presently took up a book, and after that went to her own room, where she stood awhile at her window, and looked out on the garden of the Ursulines. The moon hung full orb in the stainless heaven, and deepened the mystery of the paths and trees, and lit the silvery roofs and chimneys of the convent with tender effulgence. A wandering odor of leaf and flower stole up from the garden, but she perceived the sweetness, like the splendor, with veiled senses. She was turning over in her thought the incidents of her walk, and trying to make out if anything had really happened, first to provoke her against Mr. Arbuton, and then to reconcile her to him. Had he said or done anything about her favorite painting (which she hated now), or the Marches, to offend her? Or if it had been his tone and manner, was his after-conduct at the old church sufficient penance? What was it he had done that common humanity did not require? Was he so very superior to common humanity, that she should meekly rejoice at his kindness to the afflicted mother? Why need she have cared for his forbearance toward the rapt devotee? She became aware that she was ridiculous. "Dick was right," she confessed, "and I will *not* let myself be made a goose of"; and when the bugle at the citadel called the soldiers to rest, and the harsh chapel-bell bade the nuns go dream of heaven, she also fell asleep, a smile on her lips and a light heart in her breast.

W. D. Howells

VI

A LETTER OF KITTY'S

Quebec, August—, 1870.

Dear Girls: Since the letter I wrote you a day or two after we got here, we have been going on very much as you might have expected. A whole week has passed, but we still bear our enforced leisure with fortitude; and, though Boston and New York are both fading into the improbable (as far as we are concerned), Quebec continues inexhaustible, and I don't begrudge a moment of the time we are giving it.

Fanny still keeps her sofa; the first enthusiasm of her affliction has worn away, and she has nothing to sustain her now but planning our expeditions about the city. She has got the map and the history of Quebec by heart, and she holds us to the literal fulfilment of her instructions. On this account, she often has to send Dick and me out together when she would like to keep him with her, for she won't trust either of us alone, and when we come back she examines us separately to see whether we have skipped anything. This makes us faithful in the smallest things. She says she is determined that Uncle Jack shall have a full and circumstantial report from me of all that he wants to know about the celebrated places here, and I really think he will, if I go on, or am goaded on, in this way. It's pure devotion to the cause in Fanny, for you know she doesn't care for such things herself, and has no pleasure in it but carrying a point. Her chief consolation under her trial of keeping still is to see how I look in her different dresses. She sighs over me as I appear in a new garment, and says, O, if she only had the dressing of me! Then she gets up and limps and hops across the room to where I stand before the glass, and puts a pin here and a ribbon there, and gives my hair (which she has dressed herself) a little dab, to make it lie differently, and then scrambles back to her sofa, and knocks her lame ankle against something, and lies there groaning and enjoying herself like a martyr. On days when she thinks she is never going to get well, she says she doesn't know why she doesn't give me her things at once and be done with it; and on days when she thinks she is going to get well right away, she says she will have me one made something like whatever dress I have got on, as soon as she's home. Then up she'll jump again for the exact measure, and tell me the history of every stitch, and how she'll have it altered just the least grain, and differently trimmed to suit my complexion better; and ends by having promised to get me something not in the least like it. You have some idea already of what Fanny is; and all you have got to do is to multiply it by about fifty thousand. Her sprained ankle simply intensifies her whole character.

Besides helping to compose Fanny's expeditionary corps, and really exerting himself in the cause of Uncle Jack, as he calls it, Dick is behaving beautifully. Every morning, after breakfast, he goes over to the hotel, and looks at the arrivals and reads the newspapers, and though we never get anything out of him afterwards, we somehow feel informed of all that is going on. He has taken to smoking a clay pipe in honor of the Canadian fashion, and he wears a gay, barbaric scarf of Indian muslin wound round his hat and flying out behind; because the Quebeckers protect them-selves in that way against sunstroke when the thermometer gets up among the sixties. He has also bought a pair of snow-shoes to be prepared for the other extreme of weather, in case anything else should happen to Fanny, and detain us into the winter. When he has rested from his walk to the hotel, we usually go out together and explore, as we do also in the afternoon; and in the evening we walk on Durham Terrace,—a promenade overlooking the river, where the whole cramped and crooked city goes for exercise. It's a formal parade in the evening; but one morning I went there before breakfast, for a change, and found it the resort of careless ease; two or three idle boys were sunning themselves on the carriages of the big guns that stand on the Terrace, a little dog was barking at the chimneys of the Lower Town, and an old gentleman was walking up and down in his dressing-gown and slippers, just as if it were his own front porch. He looked something like Uncle Jack, and I wished it had been he,—to see the smoke curling softly up from the Lower Town, the bustle about the market-place, and the shipping in the river, and the haze hanging over the water a little way off, and the near hills all silver, and the distant ones blue.

But if we are coming to the grand and the beautiful, why, there is no direction in which you can look about Quebec without seeing it; and it is always mixed up with something so familiar and homelike, that my heart warms to it. The Jesuit Barracks are just across the street from us in the foreground of the most magnificent landscape; the building is—think, you Eriecreekers of an hour!—two hundred years old, and it looks five hundred. The English took it away from the Jesuits in 1760, and have used it as barracks ever since; but it isn't in the least changed, so that a Jesuit missionary who visited it the other day said that it was as if his brother priests had been driven out of it the week before. Well, you might think so old and so historical a place would be putting on airs, but it takes as kindly to domestic life as a new frame-house, and I am never tired of looking over into the yard at the frowsy soldiers' wives hanging out clothes, and the unkempt children playing among the burdocks, and chickens and cats, and the soldiers themselves carrying about the officers' boots, or sawing wood and picking up chips to boil the teakettle.

They are off dignity as well as off duty, then; but when they are on both, and in full dress, they make our volunteers (as I remember them) seem very shabby and slovenly.

Over the belfry of the Barracks, our windows command a view of half Quebec, with its roofs and spires dropping down the slope to the Lower Town, where the masts of the ships in the river come tapering up among them, and then of the plain stretching from the river in the valley to a range of mountains against the horizon, with far-off white villages glimmering out of their purple folds. The whole plain is bright with houses and harvest-fields; and the distinctly divided farms—the owners cut them up every generation, and give each son a strip of the entire length—run back on either hand, from the straight roads bordered by poplars, while the highways near the city pass between lovely villas.

But this landscape and the Jesuit Barracks, with all their merits, are nothing to the Ursuline Convent, just under our back windows, which I told you something about in my other letter. We have been reading up its history since, and we know about Madame de la Peltrie, the noble Norman lady who founded it in 1640. She was very rich and very beautiful, and a saint from the beginning, so that when her husband died, and her poor old father wanted her to marry again and not go into a nunnery, she didn't mind cheating him by a sham marriage with a devout gentleman; and she came to Canada as soon as her father was dead, with another saint, Marie de l'Incarnation, and founded this convent. The first building is standing yet, as strong as ever, though everything but the stone walls was burnt two centuries ago. Only a few years since an old ash-tree, under which the Ursulines first taught the Indian children, blew down, and now a large black cross marks its place. The modern nuns are in the garden nearly the whole morning long, and by night the ghosts of the former nuns haunt it; and in very bright moonlight I myself do a bit of Madame de la Peltrie there, and teach little Indian boys, who dwindle like those in the song, as the moon goes down. It is

W. D. Howells

an enchanted place, and I wish we had it in the back yard at Eriecreek, though I don't think the neighbors would approve of the architecture. I have adopted two nuns for my own: one is tall and slender and pallid, and you can see at a glance that she broke the heart of a mortal lover, and knew it, when she became the bride of heaven; and the other is short and plain and plump, and looks as comfortable and commonplace as life-after-dinner. When the world is bright I revel in the statue-like sadness of the beautiful nun, who never laughs or plays with the little girl pupils; but when the world is dark—as the best of worlds will be at times for a minute or two—I take to the fat nun, and go in for a clumsy romp with the children; and then I fancy that I am wiser if not better than the fair slim Ursuline. But whichever I am, for the time being, I am vexed with the other; yet they always are together, as if they were counterparts. I think a nice story might be written about them.

In Wolfe's siege of Quebec this Ursuline Garden of ours was everywhere torn up by the falling bombs, and the sisters were driven out into the world they had forsaken forever, as Fanny has been reading in a little French account of the events, written at the time, by a nun of the General Hospital. It was there the Ursulines took what refuge there was; going from their cloistered school-rooms and their innocent little ones to the wards of the hospital, filled with the wounded and dying of either side, and echoing with their dreadful groans. What a sad, evil, bewildering world they had a glimpse of! In the garden here, our poor Montcalm—I belong to the French side, please, in Quebec—was buried in a grave dug for him by a bursting shell. They have his skull now in the chaplain's room of the convent, where we saw it the other day. They have made it comfortable in a glass box, neatly bound with black, and covered with a white lace drapery, just as if it were a saint's. It was broken a little in taking it out of the grave; and a few years ago, some English officers borrowed it to look at, and were horrible enough to pull out some of the teeth. Tell Uncle Jack the head is very broad above the ears, but the forehead is small.

The chaplain also showed us a copy of an old painting of the first convent, Indian lodges, Madame de la Peltrie's house, and Madame herself, very splendidly dressed, with an Indian chief before her, and some French cavaliers riding down an avenue towards her. Then he showed us some of the nuns' work in albums, painted and lettered in a way to give me an idea of old missals. By and by he went into the chapel with us, and it gave such a queer notion of his indoors life to have him put on an overcoat and india-rubbers to go a few rods through the open air to the chapel door: he had not been very well, he said. When he got in, he took off his hat, and put on an octagonal priest's cap, and showed us everything in the kindest way—and his manners were exquisite. There were beautiful paintings sent out from France at the time of the Revolution; and wood-carvings round the high-altar, done by Quebec artists in the beginning of the last century; for he said they had a school of arts then at St. Anne's, twenty miles below the city. Then there was an ivory crucifix, so life-like that you could scarcely bear to look at it. But what I most cared for was the tiny twinkle of a votive lamp which he pointed out to us in one corner of the nuns' chapel: it was lit a hundred and fifty years ago by two of our French officers when their sister took the veil, and has never been extinguished since, except during the siege of 1759. Of course, I think a story might be written about *this*; and the truth is, the possibilities of fiction in Quebec are overpowering; I go about in a perfect haze of romances, and meet people at every turn who have nothing to do but invite the passing novelist into their houses, and have their likenesses done at once for heroes and heroines. They needn't change a thing about them, but sit just as they are; and if this is in the present, only think how the whole past of Quebec must be crying out to be put into historical romances!

I wish you could see the houses, and how substantial they

are. I can only think of Eriecreek as an assemblage of huts and bark-lodges in contrast. Our boarding-house is comparatively slight, and has stone walls only a foot and a half thick, but the average is two feet and two and a half; and the other day Dick went through the Laval University,—he goes everywhere and gets acquainted with everybody,—and saw the foundation walls of the first building, which have stood all the sieges and conflagrations since the seventeenth century; and no wonder, for they are six feet thick, and form a series of low-vaulted corridors, as heavy, he says, as the casemates of a fortress. There is a beautiful old carved staircase there, of the same date; and he liked the president, a priest, ever so much; and we like the looks of all the priests we see; they are so handsome and polite, and they all speak English, with some funny little defect. The other day, we asked such a nice young priest about the way to Hare Point, where it is said the Recollet friars had their first mission on the marshy meadows: he didn't know of this bit of history, and we showed him our book. "Ah! you see, the book say 'pro-*bab*-ly the site.' If it had said *certainly*, I should have known. But pro-*bab*-ly, pro-*bab*-ly, you see!" However, he showed us the way, and down we went through the Lower Town, and out past the General Hospital to this Pointe aux Lievres, which is famous also because somewhere near it, on the St. Charles, Jacques Cartier wintered in 1536, and kidnapped the Indian king Donnacona, whom he carried to France. And it was here Montcalm's forces tried to rally after their defeat by Wolfe. (Please read this several times to Uncle Jack, so that he can have it impressed upon him how faithful I am in my historical researches.)

It makes me dreadfully angry and sad to think the French should have been robbed of Quebec, after what they did to build it. But it is still quite a French city in everything, even to sympathy with France in this Prussian war, which you would hardly think they would care about. Our landlady says the very boys in the street know about the battles, and explain, every time the French are beaten, how they were outnumbered and betrayed,—something the way we used to do in the first of our war.

I suppose you will think I am crazy; but I do wish Uncle Jack would wind up his practice at Eriecreek, and sell the house, and come to live at Quebec. I have been asking prices of things, and I find that everything is very cheap, even according to the Eriecreek standard; we could get a beautiful house on the St. Louis Road for two hundred a year; beef is ten or twelve cents a pound, and everything else in proportion. Then besides that, the washing is sent out into the country to be done by the peasant-women, and there isn't a crumb of bread baked in the house, but it all comes from the bakers; and only think, girls, what a relief that would be! Do get Uncle Jack to consider it *seriously*.

Since I began this letter the afternoon has worn away—the light from the sunset on the mountains would glorify our supper-table without extra charge, if we lived here—and the twilight has passed, and the moon has come up over the gables and dormer-windows of the convent, and looks into the garden so invitingly that I can't help joining her. So I will put my writing by till to-morrow. The going-to-bed bell has rung, and the red lights have vanished one by one from the windows, and the nuns are asleep, and another set of ghosts is playing in the garden with the copper-colored phantoms of the Indian children of long ago. What! not Madame de la Peltrie? Oh! how do they like those little fibs of yours up in heaven?

Sunday afternoon.—As we were at the French cathedral last Sunday, we went to the English to-day; and I could easily have imagined myself in some church of Old England, hearing the royal family prayed for, and listening to the pretty poor sermon delivered with such an English *brogue*. The people, too, had such Englishy faces and such queer little eccentricities of dress; the young lady that sang contralto in the choir wore a scarf like a man's on her hat. The cathedral isn't much, architecturally, I suppose, but it affected me very solemnly, and I couldn't help feeling that it was as much a part of British power and grandeur as the citadel itself. Over the bishop's seat drooped the flag of a Crimean regiment, tattered by time and battles, which was hung up here with great ceremonies, in 1860, when the Prince of Wales presented them with new colors; and up in the gallery was a kind of glorified pew for royal highnesses and governor-generals and so forth, to sit in when they are here. There are tablets and monumental busts about the walls; and one to the memory of the Duke of Lenox, the governor-general who died in the middle of the last century from the bite of a fox; which seemed an odd fate for a duke, and somehow made me very sorry for him.

Fanny, of course, couldn't go to church with me, and Dick got out of it by lingering too late over the newspapers at the hotel, and so I trudged off with our Bostonian, who is still with us here. I didn't dwell much upon him in my last letter, and I don't believe now I can make him quite clear to you. He has been a good deal abroad, and he is Europeanized enough not to think much of America, though I can't find that he quite approves of Europe, and his experience seems not to have left him any particular country in either hemisphere.

He isn't the Bostonian of Uncle Jack's imagination, and I suspect he wouldn't like to be. He is rather too young, still, to have much of an antislavery record, and even if he had lived soon enough, I think that he would not have been a John Brown man. I am afraid that he believes in "vulgar and meretricious distinctions" of all sorts, and that he hasn't an atom of "magnanimous democracy" in him. In fact, I find, to my great astonishment, that some ideas which I thought were held only in England, and which I had never seriously thought of, seem actually a part of Mr. Arbuton's nature or education. He talks about the lower classes, and tradesmen, and the best people, and good families, as I supposed nobody in *this* country *ever* did,—in earnest. To be sure, I have always been reading of characters who had such opinions, but I thought they were just put into novels to eke out somebody's unhappiness,—to keep the high-born daughter from marrying beneath her for love, and so on; or else to be made fun of in the person of some silly old woman or some odious snob; and I could hardly believe at first that our Bostonian was serious in talking in that way. Such things sound so differently in real life; and I laughed at them till I found that he didn't know what to make of my laughing, and then I took leave to differ with him in some of his notions; but he never disputes anything I say, and so makes it seem rude to differ with him. I always feel, though he begins it, as if I had thrust my opinions upon him. But in spite of his weaknesses and disagreeabilities, there is something really *high* about him; he is so scrupulously true, so exactly just, that Uncle Jack himself couldn't be more so; though you can see that he respects his virtues as the peculiar result of some extraordinary system. Here at Quebec, though he goes round patronizing the landscape and the antiquities, and coldly smiling at my little enthusiasms, there is really a great deal that ought to be at least improving in him. I get to paying him the same respect that he pays himself, and imbues his very clothes with, till everything he has on appears to look like him and respect itself accordingly. I have often wondered what his hat, his honored hat, for instance, would do, if I should throw it out of the front window. It would make an earthquake, I believe.

He is politely curious about us; and from time to time, in a shrinking, disgusted way, he asks some leading question about Eriecreek, which he doesn't seem able to form any idea of, as much as I explain it. He clings to his original notion, that it is in the heart of the Oil Regions, of which he has seen pictures in the illustrated papers; and when I assert myself against his opinions, he treats me very gingerly, as if I were an explosive sprite, or an inflammable naiad from a torpedoed well, and it wouldn't be quite safe to oppose me, or I would disappear with a flash and a bang.

W. D. Howells

When Dick isn't able to go with me on Fanny's account, Mr. Arbuton takes his place in the expeditionary corps; and we have visited a good many points of interest together, and now and then he talks very entertainingly about his travels. But I don't think they have made him very cosmopolitan. It seems as if he went about with a little imaginary standard, and was chiefly interested in things, to see whether they fitted it or not. Trifling matters annoy him; and when he finds sublimity mixed up with absurdity, it almost makes him angry. One of the oddest and oldest-looking buildings in Quebec is a little one-story house on St. Louis Street, to which poor General Montgomery was taken after he was shot; and it is a pastry-cook's now, and the tarts and cakes in the window vexed Mr. Arbuton so much—not that he seemed to care for Montgomery—that I didn't dare to laugh.

I live very little in the nineteenth century at present, and do not care much for people who do. Still I have a few grains of affection left for Uncle Jack, which I want you to give him.

I suppose it will take about six stamps to pay this letter. I forgot to say that Dick goes to be barbered every day at the "Montcalm Shaving and Shampooing Saloon," so called because they say Montcalm held his last council of war there. It is a queer little steep-roofed house, with a flowering bean up the front, and a bit of garden, full of snap-dragons, before it.

We shall be here a week or so yet, at any rate, and then, I think, we shall go straight home, Dick has lost so much time already.

With a great deal of love,

Your Kitty.

VII

LOVE'S YOUNG DREAM

With the two young people whose days now lapsed away together, it could not be said that Monday varied much from Tuesday, or ten o'clock from half past three; they were not always certain what day of the week it was, and sometimes they fancied that a thing which happened in the morning had taken place yesterday afternoon.

But whatever it was, and however uncertain in time and character their slight adventure was to themselves, Mrs. Ellison secured all possible knowledge of it from Kitty. Since it was her misfortune that promoted it, she considered herself a martyr to Kitty's acquaintance with Mr. Arbuton, and believed that she had the best claim to any gossip that could come of it. She lounged upon her sofa, and listened with a patience superior to the maiden caprice with which her inquisition was sometimes met; for if that delayed her satisfaction it also employed her arts, and the final triumph of getting everything out of Kitty afforded her a delicate self-flattery. But commonly the young girl was ready enough to speak, for she was glad to have the light of a worldlier mind and a greater experience than her own on Mr. Arbuton's character: if Mrs. Ellison was not the wisest head, still talking him over was at least a relief from thinking him over; and then, at the end of the ends, when were ever two women averse to talk of a man?

She commonly sought Fanny's sofa when she returned from

W. D. Howells

her rambles through the city, and gave a sufficiently strict account of what had happened. This was done light-heartedly and with touches of burlesque and extravagance at first; but the reports grew presently to have a more serious tone, and latterly Kitty had been so absent at times that she would fall into a puzzled silence in the midst of her narration; or else she would meet a long procession of skilfully marshalled questions with a flippancy that no one but a martyr could have suffered. But Mrs. Ellison bore all and would have borne much more in that cause. Battled at one point, she turned to another, and the sum of her researches was often a clearer perception of Kitty's state of mind than the young girl herself possessed. For her, indeed, the whole affair was full of mystery and misgiving.

"Our acquaintance has the charm of novelty every time we meet," she said once, when pressed hard by Mrs. Ellison. "We are growing better strangers, Mr. Arbuton and I. By and by, some morning, we shall not know each other by sight. I can barely recognize him now, though I thought I knew him pretty well once. I want you to understand that I speak as an unbiassed spectator, Fanny."

"O Kitty! how can you accuse me of trying to pry into your affairs!" cries injured Mrs. Ellison, and settles herself in a more comfortable posture for listening.

"I don't accuse you of anything. I'm sure you've a right to know everything about me. Only, I want you really to know."

"Yes, dear," says the matron, with hypocritical meekness.

"Well," resumes Kitty, "there are things that puzzle me more and more about him,—things that used to amuse me at first, because I didn't actually believe that they could be, and that I felt like defying afterwards. But now I can't bear up against them. They frighten me, and seem to deny me the right to be what I believe I am."

"I don't understand you, Kitty."

"Why, you've seen how it is with us at home, and how Uncle Jack has brought us up. We never had a rule for anything except to do what was right, and to be careful of the rights of others."

"Well."

"Well, Mr. Arbuton seems to have lived in a world where everything is regulated by some rigid law that it would be death to break. Then, you know, at home we are always talking about people, and discussing them; but we always talk of each person for what he is in himself, and I always thought a person could refine himself if he tried, and was sincere, and not conceited. But *he* seems to judge people according to their origin and locality and calling, and to believe that all refinement must come from just such training and circumstances as his own. Without exactly saying so, he puts everything else quite out of the question. He doesn't appear to dream that there can be any different opinion. He tramples upon all that I have been taught to believe; and though I cling the closer to my idols, I can't help, now and then, trying myself by his criterions; and then I find myself wanting in every civilized trait, and my whole life coarse and poor, and all my associations hopelessly degraded. I think his ideas are hard and narrow, and I believe that even my little experience would prove them false; but then, they are his, and I can't reconcile them with what I see is good in him."

Kitty spoke with half-averted face where she sat beside one of the front windows, looking absently out on the distant line of violet hills beyond Charlesbourg, and now and then lifting her glove from her lap and letting it drop again.

"Kitty," said Mrs. Ellison in reply to her difficulties, "you oughtn't to sit against a light like that. It makes your profile quite black to any one back in the room."

"O well, Fanny, I'm not black in reality."

"Yes, but a young lady ought always to think how she is looking. Suppose some one was to come in."

"Dick's the only one likely to come in just now, and he wouldn't mind it. But if you like it better, I'll come and sit by you," said Kitty, and took her place beside the sofa.

Her hat was in her hand, her sack on her arm; the fatigue of a recent walk gave her a soft pallor, and languor of face and attitude. Mrs. Ellison admired her pretty looks with a generous regret that they should be wasted on herself, and then asked, "Where were you this afternoon?"

"O, we went to the Hotel Dieu, for one thing, and afterwards we looked into the court-yard of the convent; and there another of his pleasant little traits came out,—a way he has of always putting you in the wrong even when it's a matter of no consequence any way, and there needn't be any right or wrong about it. I remembered the place because Mrs. March, you know, showed us a rose that one of the nuns in the hospital gave her, and I tried to tell Mr. Arbuton about it, and he graciously took it as if poor Mrs. March had made an advance towards his acquaintance. I do wish you could see what a lovely place that court-yard is, Fanny. It's so strange that such a thing should be right there, in the heart of this crowded city; but there it was, with its peasant cottage on one side, and its long, low barns on the other, and those wide-horned Canadian cows munching at the racks of hay outside, and pigeons and chickens all about among their feet—"

"Yes, yes; never mind all that, Kitty. You know I hate nature. Go on about Mr. Arbuton," said Mrs. Ellison, who did not mean a sarcasm.

"It looked like a farmyard in a picture, far out in the country somewhere," resumed Kitty; "and Mr. Arbuton did it the honor to say it was just like Normandy."

"Kitty!"

"He did, indeed, Fanny; and the cows didn't go down on their knees out of gratitude, either. Well, off on the right were the hospital buildings climbing up, you know, with their stone walls and steep roofs, and windows dropped about over them, like our convent here; and there was an artist there, sketching it all; he had such a brown, pleasant face, with a little black mustache and imperial, and such gay black eyes that nobody could help falling in love with him; and he was talking in such a free-and-easy way with the lazy workmen and women overlooking him. He jotted down a little image of the Virgin in a niche on the wall, and one of the people called out,—Mr. Arbuton was translating,—'Look there! with one touch he's made our Blessed Lady.' 'O,' says the painter, 'that's nothing; with three touches I can make the entire Holy Family.' And they all laughed; and that little joke, you know, won my heart,—I don't hear many jokes from Mr. Arbuton;—and so I said what a blessed life a painter's must be, for it would give you a right to be a vagrant, and you could wander through the world, seeing everything that was lovely and funny, and nobody could blame you; and I wondered everybody who had the chance didn't learn to sketch. Mr. Arbuton took it seriously, and said people had to have something more than the chance to learn before they could sketch, and that most of them were an affliction with their sketchbooks, and he had seen too much of the sad effects of drawing from casts. And he put me in the wrong, as he always does. Don't you see? I didn't want to learn drawing; I wanted to be a painter, and go about sketching beautiful old convents, and sit on camp-stools on pleasant afternoons, and joke with people. Of course, he couldn't understand that. But I know the artist could. O Fanny, if it had only been the painter whose arm I took that first day on the boat, instead of Mr. Arbuton! But the worst of it is, he is making a hypocrite of me, and a cowardly, unnatural girl. I wanted to go nearer and look at the painter's sketch; but I was ashamed to say I'd never seen a real artist's sketch before, and I'm getting to be ashamed, or to seem ashamed, of a great many innocent things. He has a way of not seeming to think it possible that any one he associates with can differ from him. And I do differ from him. I differ from him as much as my whole past life differs from his; I know I'm just the kind of production that he disapproves of, and that I'm altogether irregular and unauthorized and unjustifiable; and though it's funny to have him talking to me as if I must have the sympathy of a rich girl with his ideas, it's provoking, too, and it's very bad for me. Up to the present moment, Fanny, if you want to know, that's the principal effect of Mr. Arbuton on me. I'm being gradually snubbed and scared into treasons, stratagems, and spoils."

Mrs. Ellison did not find all this so very grievous, for she was one of those women who like a snub from the superior sex, if it does not involve a slight to their beauty or their power of pleasing. But she thought it best not to enter into the question, and merely said, "But surely, Kitty, there are a great many things in Mr. Arbuton that you must respect."

"Respect? O, yes, indeed! But respect isn't just the thing for one who seems to consider himself sacred. Say *revere*, Fanny; say revere!"

Kitty had risen from her chair, but Mrs. Ellison waved her again to her seat with an imploring gesture. "Don't go, Kitty; I'm not half done with you yet. You *must* tell me something more. You've stirred me up so, now. I know you don't always have such disagreeable times. You've often come home quite happy. What do you generally find to talk about? Do tell me some particulars for once."

"Why, little topics come up, you know. But sometimes we don't talk at all, because I don't like to say what I think or feel, for fear I should be thinking or feeling something vulgar. Mr. Arbuton is rather a blight upon conversation in that way. He makes you doubtful whether there isn't something a little common in breathing and the circulation of the blood, and whether it wouldn't be true refinement to stop them."

"Stuff, Kitty! He's very cultivated, isn't he? Don't you talk about books? He's read everything, I suppose."

"O yes, he's *read* enough."

"What do you mean?"

"Nothing. Only sometimes it seems to me as if he hadn't read because he loved it, but because he thought it due to himself. But maybe I'm mistaken. I could imagine a delicate poem shutting up half its sweetness from his cold, cold scrutiny,—if you will excuse the floweriness of the idea."

"Why, Kitty! don't you think he's refined? I'm sure, I think he's a *very* refined person."

"He's a very elaborated person. But I don't think it would make much difference to him what our opinion of him was. His own good opinion would be quite enough."

"Is he—is he—always agreeable?"

"I thought we were discussing his mind, Fanny. I don't know that I feel like enlarging upon his manners," said Kitty, slyly.

"But surely, Kitty," said the matron, with an air of argument, "there's some connection between his mind and his manners."

"Yes, I suppose so. I don't think there's much between his heart and his manners. They seem to have been put on him instead of having come out of him. He's very well trained, and nine times out of ten he's so exquisitely polite that it's wonderful; but the tenth time he may say something so rude that you can't believe it."

"Then you like him nine times out of ten."

"I didn't say that. But for the tenth time, it's certain, his training doesn't hold out, and he seems to have nothing natural to fall back upon. But you can believe that, if he knew he'd been disagreeable, he'd be sorry for it."

W. D. Howells

"Why, then, Kitty, how can you say that there's no connection between his heart and manners? This very thing proves that they come from his heart. Don't be illogical, Kitty," said Mrs. Ellison, and her nerves added, *sotto voce*, "if you *are* so abominably provoking!"

"O," responded the young girl, with the kind of laugh that meant it was, after all, not such a laughing matter, "I didn't say he'd be sorry for *you*! Perhaps he would; but he'd be certain to be sorry for himself. It's with his politeness as it is with his reading; he seems to consider it something that's due to himself as a gentleman to treat people well; and it isn't in the least as if he cared for *them*. He wouldn't like to fail in such a point."

"But, Kitty, isn't that to his credit?"

"Maybe. I don't say. If I knew more about the world, perhaps I should admire it. But now, you see,"—and here Kitty's laugh grew more natural, and she gave a subtle caricature of Mr. Arbuton's air and tone as she spoke,—"I can't help feeling that it's a little—vulgar."

Mrs. Ellison could not quite make out how much Kitty really meant of what she had said. She gasped once or twice for argument; then she sat up, and beat the sofa-pillows vengefully in composing herself anew, and finally, "Well, Kitty, I'm sure I don't know what to make of it all," she said with a sigh.

"Why, we're not obliged to make anything of it, Fanny, there's that comfort," replied Kitty; and then there was a silence, while she brooded over the whole affair of her acquaintance with Mr. Arbuton, which this talk had failed to set in a more pleasant or hopeful light. It had begun like a romance; she had pleased her fancy, if not her heart, with the poetry of it; but at last she felt exiled and strange in his presence. She had no right to a different result, even through any deep feeling in the matter; but while she owned, with her half-sad, half-comical consciousness, that she had been tacitly claiming and expecting too much, she softly pitied herself, with a kind of impersonal compassion, as if it were some other girl whose pretty dream had been broken. Its ruin involved the loss of another ideal; for she was aware that there had been gradually rising in her mind an image of Boston, different alike from the holy place of her childhood, the sacred city of the antislavery heroes and martyrs, and from the jesting, easy, sympathetic Boston of Mr. and Mrs. March. This new Boston with which Mr. Arbuton inspired her was a Boston of mysterious prejudices and lofty reservations; a Boston of high and difficult tastes, that found its social ideal in the Old World, and that shrank from contact with the reality of this; a Boston as alien as Europe to her simple experiences, and that seemed to be proud only of the things that were unlike other American things; a Boston that would rather perish by fire and sword than be suspected of vulgarity; a critical, fastidious, and reluctant Boston, dissatisfied with the rest of the hemisphere, and gelidly self-satisfied in so far as it was not in the least the Boston of her fond preconceptions. It was, doubtless, no more the real Boston we know and love, than either of the others: and it perplexed her more than it need, even if it had not been mere phantasm. It made her suspicious of Mr. Arbuton's behavior towards her, and observant of little things that might very well have otherwise escaped her. The bantering humor, the light-hearted trust and self-reliance with which she had once met him deserted her, and only returned fitfully when some accident called her out of herself, and made her forget the differences that she now too plainly saw in their ways of thinking and feeling. It was a greater and greater effort to place herself in sympathy with him; she relaxed into a languid self-contempt, as if she had been playing a part, when she succeeded. "Sometimes, Fanny," she said, now, after a long pause, speaking in behalf of that other girl she had been thinking of, "it seems to me as if Mr. Arbuton were all gloves and slim umbrella,—the mere husk of well dressed culture and good manners. His looks *do* promise everything; but O dear me! I should be sorry for any one that was in love with him. Just imagine some girl meeting with such a man, and taking a fancy to him! I suppose she never would quite believe but that he must somehow be what she first thought him, and she would go down to her grave believing that she had failed to understand him. What a curious story it would make!"

"Then, why don't you write it, Kitty?" asked Mrs. Ellison. "No one could do it better."

Kitty flushed quickly; then she smiled: "O, I don't think I could do it at all. It wouldn't be a very easy story to work out. Perhaps he might never do anything positively disagreeable enough to make anybody condemn him. The only way you could show his character would be to have her do and say hateful things to him, when she couldn't help it, and then repent of it, while he was impassively perfect through everything. And perhaps, after all, he might be regarded by some stupid people as the injured one. Well, Mr. Arbuton has been very polite to us, I'm sure, Fanny," she said after another pause, as she rose from her chair, "and maybe I'm unjust to him. I beg his pardon of you; and I wish," she added with a dull disappointment quite her own, and a pang of surprise at words that seemed to utter themselves, "that he would go away."

"Why, Kitty, I'm shocked," said Mrs. Ellison, rising from her cushions.

"Yes; so am I, Fanny."

"Are you really tired of him, then?"

Kitty did not answer, but turned away her face a little, where she stood beside the chair in which she had been sitting.

Mrs. Ellison put out her hand towards her. "Kitty, come here," she said with imperious tenderness.

"No, I won't, Fanny," answered the young girl, in a trembling voice. She raised the glove that she had been nervously swinging back and forth, and bit hard upon the button of it. "I don't know whether I'm tired of *him*,—though he isn't a person to rest one a great deal,—but I'm tired of *it*. I'm perplexed and troubled the whole time, and I don't see any end to it. Yes, I wish he would go away! Yes, he *is* tiresome. What is he staying here for? If he thinks himself so much better than all of us, I wonder he troubles himself with our company. It's quite time for him to go. No, Fanny, no," cried Kitty with a little broken laugh, still rejecting the outstretched hand, "I'll be flat in private, if you please." And dashing her hand across her eyes, she flitted out of the room. At the door she turned and said,

"You needn't think it's what you think it is, Fanny."

"No indeed, dear; you're just overwrought."

"For I really wish he'd go."

But it was on this very day that Mr. Arbuton found it harder than ever to renew his resolution of quitting Quebec, and cutting short at once his acquaintance with these people. He had been pledging himself to this in some form every day, and every morrow had melted his resolution away. Whatever was his opinion of Colonel and Mrs. Ellison, it is certain that, if he considered Kitty merely in relation to the present, he could not have said how, by being different, she could have been better than she was. He perceived a charm, that would be recognized anywhere, in her manner, though it was not of his world; her fresh pleasure in all she saw, though he did not know how to respond to it, was very winning; he respected what he thought the good sense running through her transports; he wondered at the culture she had somewhere, somehow got; and he was so good as to find that her literary enthusiasms had nothing offensive, but were as pretty and naive as a girl's love of flowers. Moreover, he approved of some personal attributes of hers: a low, gentle voice, tender long-lashed eyes; a trick of drooping shoulders, and of idle hands fallen into the lap, one in the other's palm; a serene repose of face; a light and eager laugh. There was nothing so novel in those traits, and in

W. D. Howells

different combination he had seen them a thousand times; yet in her they strangely wrought upon his fancy. She had that soft, kittenish way with her which invites a caressing patronage, but, as he learned, she had also the kittenish equipment for resenting over-condescension; and she never took him half so much as when she showed the high spirit that was in her, and defied him most.

For here and now, it was all well enough; but he had a future to which he owed much, and a conscience that would not leave him at rest. The fascination of meeting her so familiarly under the same roof, the sorcery of the constant sight of her, were becoming too much; it would not do on any account; for his own sake he must put an end to it. But from hour to hour he lingered upon his unenforced resolve. The passing days, that brought him doubts in which he shuddered at the great difference between himself and her and her people, brought him also moments of blissful forgetfulness in which his misgivings were lost in the sweetness of her looks, or the young grace of her motions. Passing, the days rebuked his delay in vain; a week and two weeks slipped from under his feet, and still he had waited for fate to part him and his folly. But now at last he would go and in the evening, after his cigar on Durham Terrace, he knocked at Mrs. Ellison's door to say that on the day after to-morrow he should push on to the White Mountains.

He found the Ellisons talking over an expedition for the next morning, in which he was also to take part. Mrs. Ellison had already borne her full share in the preparation; for, being always at hand there in her room, and having nothing to do, she had been almost a willing victim to the colonel's passion for information at second-hand, and had probably come to know more than any other American woman of Arnold's expedition against Quebec in 1775. She know why the attack was planned, and with what prodigious hazard and heroical toil and endurance it was carried out; how the dauntless little army of riflemen cut their way through the untrodden forests of Maine and Canada, and beleaguered the gray old fortress on her rock till the red autumn faded into winter, and, on the last bitter night of the year, flung themselves against her defences, and fell back, leaving half their number captive, Montgomery dead, and Arnold wounded, but haplessly destined to survive.

"Yes," said the colonel, "considering the age in which they lived, and their total lack of modern improvements, mental, moral, and physical, we must acknowledge that they did pretty well. It wasn't on a very large scale; but I don't see how they could have been braver, if every man had been multiplied by ten thousand. In fact, as it's going to be all the same thing a hundred years from now, I don't know but I'd as soon be one of the men that tried to take Quebec as one of the men that did take Atlanta. Of course, for the present, and on account of my afflicted family, Mr. Arbuton, I'm willing to be what and where I am; but just see what those fellows did." And the colonel drew from his glowing memory of Mrs. Ellison's facts a brave historical picture of Arnold's expedition. "And now we're going to-morrow morning to look up the scene of the attack on the 31st of December. Kitty, sing something."

At another time Kitty might have hesitated; but that evening she was so at rest about Mr. Arbuton, so sure she cared nothing for his liking or disliking anything she did, that she sat down at the piano, and sang a number of songs, which I suppose were as unworthy the cultivated ear as any he had heard. But though they were given with an untrained voice and a touch as little skilled as might be, they pleased, or else the singer pleased. The simple-hearted courage of the performance would alone have made it charming; and Mr. Arbuton had no reason to ask himself how he should like it in Boston, if he were married, and should hear it from his wife there. Yet when a young man looks at a young girl or listens to her, a thousand vagaries possess his mind,—formless imaginations, lawless fancies. The question that presented itself remotely, like pain in a dream, dissolved in the ripple of the singer's voice, and left his revery the more luxuriously untroubled for having been.

He remembered, after saying good-night, that he had forgotten something: it was to tell them he was going away.

VIII

NEXT MORNING

Quebec lay shining in the tender oblique light of the northern sun when they passed next morning through the Upper Town market-place and took their way towards Hope Gate, where they were to be met by the colonel a little later. It is easy for the alert tourist to lose his course in Quebec, and they, who were neither hurried nor heedful, went easily astray. But the street into which they had wandered, if it did not lead straight to Hope Gate, had many merits, and was very characteristic of the city. Most of the houses on either hand were low structures of one story, built heavily of stone or stuccoed brick, with two dormer-windows, full of house-plants, in each roof; the doors were each painted of a livelier color than the rest of the house, and each glistened with a polished brass knob, a large brass knocker, or an intricate bell-pull of the same resplendent metal, and a plate bearing the owner's name and his professional title, which if not *avocat* was sure to be *notaire*, so well is Quebec supplied with those ministers of the law. At the side of each house was a *porte-cochere*, and in this a smaller door. The thresholds and doorsteps were covered with the neatest and brightest oil-cloth; the wooden sidewalk was very clean, like the steep, roughly paved street itself; and at the foot of the hill down which it sloped was a breadth of the city wall, pierced for musketry, and, past the corner of one of the houses, the half-length of cannon showing. It had the charm of those ancient streets, dear to Old-World travel, in which the past and the present, decay and repair, peace and war, have made

W. D. Howells

friends in an effect that not only wins the eye, but, however illogically, touches the heart; and over the top of the wall it had a stretch of such landscape as I know not what Old-World street can command: the St. Lawrence, blue and wide; a bit of the white village of Beauport on its bank; then a vast breadth of pale-green, upward-sloping meadows; then the purple heights; and the hazy heaven over them. Half-way down this happy street sat the artist whom they had seen before in the court of the Hotel Dieu; he was sketching something, and evoking the curious life of the neighborhood. Two schoolboys in the uniform of the Seminary paused to look at him as they loitered down the pavement; a group of children encircled him; a little girl with her hair in blue ribbons talked at a window about him to some one within; a young lady opened her casement and gazed furtively at him; a door was set quietly ajar, and an old grandam peeped out, shading her eyes with her hand; a woman in deep mourning gave his sketch a glance as she passed; a calash with a fat Quebecker in it ran into a cart driven by a broad-hatted peasant-woman, so eager were both to know what he was drawing; a man lingered even at the head of the street, as if it were any use to stop there.

As Kitty and Mr. Arbuton passed him, the artist glanced at her with the smile of a man who believes he knows how the case stands, and she followed his eye in its withdrawal towards the bit he was sketching: an old roof, and on top of this a balcony, shut in with green blinds; yet higher, a weather-worn, wood-colored gallery, pent-roofed and balustered, with a geranium showing through the balusters; a dormer-window with hook and tackle, beside an Oriental-shaped pavilion with a shining tin dome,—a picturesque confusion of forms which had been, apparently, added from time to time without design, and yet were full of harmony. The unreasonable succession of roofs had lifted the top far above the level of the surrounding houses, into the heart of the morning light, and some white doves circled about the pavilion, or nestled cooing upon the window-sill, where a young girl sat and sewed.

"Why, it's Hilda in her tower," said Kitty, "of course! And this is just the kind of street for such a girl to look down into. It doesn't seem like a street in real life, does it? The people all look as if they had stepped out of stories, and might step back any moment; and these queer little houses: they're the very places for things to happen in!"

Mr. Arbuton smiled forbearingly, as she thought, at this burst, but she did not care, and she turned, at the bottom of the street, and lingered a few moments for another look at the whole charming picture; and then he praised it, and said that the artist was making a very good sketch. "I wonder Quebec isn't infested by artists the whole summer long," he added. "They go about hungrily picking up bits of the picturesque, along our shores and country roads, when they might exchange their famine for a feast by coming here."

"I suppose there's a pleasure in finding out the small graces and beauties of the poverty-stricken subjects, that they wouldn't have in better ones, isn't there?" asked Kitty. "At any rate, if I were to write a story, I should want to take the slightest sort of plot, and lay the scene in the dullest kind of place, and then bring out all their possibilities. I'll tell you a book after my own heart: 'Details,'—just the history of a week in the life of some young people who happen together in an old New England country-house; nothing extraordinary, little, every-day things told so exquisitely, and all fading naturally away without any particular result, only the full meaning of everything brought out."

"And don't you think it's rather a sad ending for all to fade away without any particular result?" asked the young man, stricken he hardly knew how or where. "Besides, I always thought that the author of that book found too much meaning in everything. He did for men, I'm sure; but I believe women are different, and see much more than we do in a little space."

"'Why has not man a microscopic eye?
For this plain reason, man is not a fly,'

nor a woman," mocked Kitty. "Have you read his other books?"

"Yes."

"Aren't they delightful?"

"They're very well; and I always wondered he could write them. He doesn't look it."

"O, have you ever seen him?"

"He lives in Boston, you know."

"Yes, yes; but—" Kitty could not go on and say that she had not supposed authors consorted with creatures of common clay; and Mr. Arbuton, who was the constant guest of people who would have thought most authors sufficiently honored in being received among them to meet such men as he, was very far from guessing what was in her mind.

He waited a moment for her, and then said, "He's a very ordinary sort of man,—not what one would exactly call a gentleman, you know, in his belongings,—and yet his books have nothing of the shop, nothing professionally literary, about them. It seems as if almost any of us might have written them."

Kitty glanced quickly at him to see if he were jesting; but Mr. Arbuton was not easily given to irony, and he was now very much in earnest about drawing on his light overcoat, which he had hitherto carried on his arm with that scrupulous consideration for it which was not dandyism, but part of his self-respect; apparently, as an overcoat, ho cared nothing for it; as the overcoat of a man of his condition he cared everything; and now, though the sun was so bright on the open spaces, in these narrow streets the garment was comfortable.

At another time, Kitty would have enjoyed the care with which he smoothed it about his person, but this profanation of her dearest ideals made the moment serious. Her pulse quickened, and she said, "I'm afraid I can't enter into your feelings. I wasn't taught to respect the idea of a gentleman very much. I've often heard my uncle say that, at the best, it was a poor excuse for not being just honest and just brave and just kind, and a false pretence of being something more. I believe, if I were a man, I shouldn't want to be a gentleman. At any rate, I'd rather be the author of those books, which any gentleman *might* have written, than all the gentlemen who didn't, put together."

In the career of her indignation she had unconsciously hurried her companion forward so swiftly that they had reached Hope Gate as she spoke, and interrupted the revery in which Colonel Ellison, loafing up against the masonry, was contemplating the sentry in his box.

"You'd better not overheat yourself so early in the day, Kitty," said her cousin, serenely, with a glance at her flushed face; "this expedition is not going to be any joke."

Now that Prescott Gate, by which so many thousands of Americans have entered Quebec since Arnold's excursionists failed to do so, is demolished, there is nothing left so picturesque and characteristic as Hope Gate, and I doubt if anywhere in Europe there is a more mediaeval-looking bit of military architecture. The heavy stone gateway is black with age, and the gate, which has probably never been closed in our century, is of massive frame set thick with mighty bolts and spikes. The wall here sweeps along the brow of the crag on which the city is built, and a steep street drops down, by stone-parapeted curves and angles, from the Upper to the Lower Town, where, in 1775, nothing but a narrow lane bordered the St. Lawrence. A considerable breadth of land has since been won from the river, and several streets and many piers now stretch between this alley and the water; but the old Sault au Matelot still crouches and creeps along under the shelter of the city wall and the overhanging rock, which is thickly bearded with weeds and grass, and trickles with abundant moisture. It must be an ice-pit in winter, and I should think it the last spot on the continent for the summer to find; but when the summer has at last found it, the old Sault au Matelot puts on a vagabond air of Southern leisure and abandon, not to be matched anywhere out of Italy. Looking from that jutting rock near Hope Gate, behind which the defeated Americans took refuge from the fire of their enemies, the vista is almost unique for a certain scenic squalor and gypsy luxury of color: sag-roofed barns and stables, and weak-backed, sunken-chested workshops of every sort lounge along in tumble-down succession, and lean up against the cliff in every imaginable posture of worthlessness and decrepitude; light wooden galleries cross to them from the second stories of the houses which back upon the alley; and over these galleries flutters, from a labyrinth of clothes-lines, a variety of bright-colored garments of all ages, sexes, and conditions; while the footway underneath abounds in gossiping women, smoking men, idle poultry, cats, children, and large, indolent Newfoundland dogs.

"It was through this lane that Arnold's party advanced almost to the foot of Mountain Street, where they were to be joined by Montgomery's force in an attempt to surprise Prescott Gate," said the colonel, with his unerring second-hand history.

"'You that will follow me to this attempt,'

'Wait till you see the whites of their eyes, and then fire low,' and so forth. By the way, do you suppose anybody did that at Bunker Hill, Mr. Arbuton? Come, you're a Boston man. My experience is that recruits chivalrously fire into the air without waiting to see the enemy at all, let alone the whites of their eyes. Why! aren't you coming?" he asked, seeing no movement to follow in Kitty or Mr. Arbuton.

"It doesn't look very pleasant under foot, Dick," suggested Kitty.

"Well, upon my word! Is this your uncle's niece? I shall never dare to report this panic at Eriecreek."

"I can see the whole length of the alley, and there's nothing in it but chickens and domestic animals."

"Very well, as Fanny says; when Uncle Jack—he's *your* uncle—asks you about every inch of the ground that Arnold's men were demoralized over, I hope you'll know what to say."

Kitty laughed and said she should try a little invention, if her Uncle Jack came down to inches.

"All right, Kitty; you can go along St. Paul Street, there, and Mr. Arbuton and I will explore the Sault au Matelot, and come out upon you, covered with glory, at the other end."

"I hope it'll be glory," said Kitty, with a glance at the lane, "but I think it's more likely to be feathers and chopped straw.—Good by, Mr. Arbuton."

"Not in the least," answered the young man; "I'm going with you."

The colonel feigned indignant surprise, and marched briskly down the Sault au Matelot alone, while the others took their way through St. Paul Street in the same direction, amidst the bustle and business of the port, past the banks and great commercial houses, with the encounter of throngs of seafaring faces of many nations, and, at the corner of St. Peter Street, a glimpse of the national flag thrown out from the American Consulate, which intensified for untravelled Kitty her sense of remoteness from her native land. At length they turned into the street now called Sault au Matelot, into which opens the lane once bearing that name, and strolled idly along in the cool shadow, silence, and solitude of the street. She was strangely released from the constraint which Mr. Arbuton usually put upon her. A certain defiant ease filled her heart; she felt and thought whatever she liked, for the first time in many days;

while he went puzzling himself with the problem of a young lady who despised gentlemen, and yet remained charming to him.

A mighty marine smell of oakum and salt-fish was in the air, and "O," sighed Kitty, "doesn't it make you long for distant seas? Shouldn't you like to be shipwrecked for half a day or so, Mr. Arbuton?"

"Yes; yes, certainly," he replied absently, and wondered what she laughed at. The silence of the place was broken only by the noise of coopering which seemed to be going on in every other house; the solitude relieved only by the Newfoundland dogs that stretched themselves upon the thresholds of the cooper-shops. The monotony of these shops and dogs took Kitty's humor, and as they went slowly by she made a jest of them, as she used to do with things she saw.

"But here's a door without a dog!" she said, presently. "This can't be a genuine cooper-shop, of course, without a dog. O, that accounts for it, perhaps!" she added, pausing before the threshold, and glancing up at a sign—"*Academie commerciale et litteraire*"—set under an upper window. "What a curious place for a seat of learning! What do you suppose is the connection between cooper-shops and an academical education, Mr. Arbuton?"

She stood looking up at the sign that moved her mirth, and swinging her shut parasol idly to and fro, while a light of laughter played over her face.

Suddenly a shadow seemed to dart betwixt her and the open doorway, Mr. Arbuton was hurled violently against her, and, as she struggled to keep her footing under the shock, she saw him bent over a furious dog, that hung from the breast of his overcoat, while he clutched its throat with both his hands.

He met the terror of her face with a quick glance. "I beg your pardon; don't call out please," he said. But from within the shop came loud cries and maledictions, "O nom de Dieu c'est le boule-dogue du capitaine anglais!" with appalling screams for help; and a wild, uncouth little figure of a man, bareheaded, horror-eyed came flying out of the open door. He wore a cooper's apron, and he bore in one hand a red-hot iron, which, with continuous clamor, he dashed against the muzzle of the hideous brute. Without a sound the dog loosed his grip, and, dropping to the ground, fled into the obscurity of the shop as silently as he had launched himself out of it, while Kitty yet stood spell-bound, and before the crowd that the appeal of Mr. Arbuton's rescuer had summoned could see what had happened.

Mr. Arbuton lifted himself, and looked angrily round upon the gaping spectators, who began, one by one, to take in their heads from their windows and to slink back to their thresholds as if they had been guilty of something much worse than a desire to succor a human being in peril.

"Good heavens!" said Mr. Arbuton, "what an abominable scene!" His face was deadly pale, as he turned from these insolent intruders to his deliverer, whom he saluted, with a "Merci bien!" spoken in a cold, steady voice. Then he drew off his overcoat, which had been torn by the dog's teeth and irreparably dishonored in the encounter. He looked at it shuddering, with a countenance of intense disgust, and made a motion as if to hurl it into the street. But his eye again fell upon the cooper's squalid little figure, as he stood twisting his hands into his apron, and with voluble eagerness protesting that it was not his dog, but that of the English ship-captain, who had left it with him, and whom he had many a time besought to have the beast killed. Mr. Arbuton, who seemed not to hear what he was saying, or to be so absorbed in something else as not to consider whether he was to blame or not, broke in upon him in French: "You've done me the greatest service. I cannot repay you, but you must take this," he said, as he thrust a bank-note into the little man's grimy hand.

"O, but it is too much! But it is like a monsieur so brave, so—"

"Hush! It was nothing," interrupted Mr. Arbuton again. Then he threw his overcoat upon the man's shoulder. "If you will do me the pleasure to receive this also? Perhaps you can make use of it."

"Monsieur heaps me with benefits;—monsieur—" began the bewildered cooper; but Mr. Arbuton turned abruptly away from him toward Kitty, who trembled at having shared the guilt of the other spectators, and seizing her hand, he placed it on his arm, where he held it close as he strode away, leaving his deliverer planted in the middle of the sidewalk and staring after him. She scarcely dared ask him if he were hurt, as she found herself doing now with a faltering voice.

"No, I believe not," he said with a glance at the frock-coat, which was buttoned across his chest and was quite intact; and still he strode on, with a quick glance at every threshold which did not openly declare a Newfoundland dog.

It had all happened so suddenly, and in so brief a time, that she might well have failed to understand it, even if she had seen it all. It was barely intelligible to Mr. Arbuton himself, who, as Kitty had loitered mocking and laughing before the door of the shop, chanced to see the dog crouched within, and had only time to leap forward and receive the cruel brute on his breast as it flung itself at her.

He had not thought of the danger to himself in what he had done. He knew that he was unhurt, but he did not care for that; he cared only that she was safe; and as he pressed her hand tight against his heart, there passed through it a thrill of inexpressible tenderness, a quick, passionate sense of possession, a rapture as of having won her and made her his own forever, by saving her from that horrible risk. The maze in which he had but now dwelt concerning her seemed an obsolete frivolity of an alien past; all the cold doubts and hindering scruples which he had felt from the first were gone; gone all his care for his world. His world? In that supreme moment, there was no world but in the tender eyes at which he looked down with a glance which she knew not how to interpret.

She thought that his pride was deeply wounded at the ignominy of his adventure,—for she was sure he would care more for that than for the danger,—and that if she spoke of it she might add to the angry pain he felt. As they hurried along she waited for him to speak, but he did not; though always, as he looked down at her with that strange look, he seemed about to speak.

Presently she stopped, and, withdrawing her hand from his arm, she cried, "Why, we've forgotten my cousin!"

"O—yes!" said Mr. Arbuton with a vacant smile.

Looking back they saw the colonel standing on the pavement near the end of the old Sault au Matelot, with his hands in his pockets, and steadfastly staring at them. He did not relax the severity of his gaze when they returned to join him, and appeared to find little consolation in Kitty's "O Dick, I forgot all about you," given with a sudden, inexplicable laugh, interrupted and renewed as some ludicrous image seemed to come and go in her mind.

"Well, this may be very flattering, Kitty, but it isn't altogether comprehensible," said he, with a keen glance at both their faces. "I don't know what you'll say to Uncle Jack. It's not forgetting me alone: it's forgetting the whole American expedition against Quebec."

The colonel waited for some reply; but Kitty dared not attempt an explanation, and Mr. Arbuton was not the man to seem to boast of his share of the adventure by telling what had happened, even if he had cared at that moment to do so. Her very ignorance of what he had dared for her only confirmed his new sense of possession; and, if he could, he would not have marred the pleasure he felt by making her grateful yet, sweet as that might be in its time. Now he liked to keep his knowledge, to have had her unwitting compassion, to hear her pour out her unwitting relief in this laugh, while he superiorly permitted it.

"I don't understand this thing," said the colonel, through whose dense, masculine intelligence some suspicions of love-making were beginning to pierce. But he dismissed them as absurd, and added, "However, I'm willing to forgive, and you've done the forgetting; and all that I ask now is the pleasure of your company on the spot where Montgomery fell. Fanny'll never believe I've found it unless you go with me," he appealed, finally.

"O, we'll go, by all means," said Mr. Arbuton, unconsciously speaking, as by authority, for both.

They came into busier streets of the Port again, and then passed through the square of the Lower Town Market, with the market-house in the midst, the shops and warehouses on either side, the long row of tented booths with every kind of peasant-wares to sell, and the wide stairway dropping to the river which brought the abundance of the neighboring country to the mart. The whole place was alive with country-folk in carts and citizens on foot. At one point a gayly painted wagon was drawn up in the midst of a group of people to whom a quackish-faced Yankee was hawking, in his own personal French, an American patent-medicine, and making his audience giggle. Because Kitty was amused at this, Mr. Arbuton found it the drollest thing imaginable, but saw something yet droller when she made the colonel look at a peasant, standing in one corner beside a basket of fowls, which a woman, coming up to buy, examined as if the provision were some natural curiosity, while a crowd at once gathered round.

"It requires a considerable population to make a bargain, up here," remarked the colonel. "I suppose they turn out the garrison when they sell a beef." For both buyer and seller seemed to take advice of the bystanders, who discussed and inspected the different fowls as if nothing so novel as poultry had yet fallen in their way.

At last the peasant himself took up the fowls and carefully scrutinized them.

"*Those* chickens, it seems, never happened to catch his eye before," interpreted Kitty; and Mr. Arbuton, who was usually very restive during such banter, smiled as if it were the most admirable fooling, or the most precious wisdom, in the world. He made them wait to see the bargain out, and could, apparently, have lingered there forever.

But the colonel had a conscience about Montgomery, and he hurried them away, on past the Queen's Wharf, and down the Cove Road to that point where the scarped and rugged breast of the cliff bears the sign, "Here fell Montgomery," though he really fell, not half-way up the height, but at the foot of it, where stood the battery that forbade his juncture with Arnold at Prescott Gate.

A certain wildness yet possesses the spot: the front of the crag, topped by the high citadel-wall, is so grim, and the few tough evergreens that cling to its clefts are torn and twisted by the winter blasts, and the houses are decrepit with age, showing here and there the scars of the frequent fires that sweep the Lower Town.

It was quite useless: neither the memories of the place nor their setting were sufficient to engage the wayward thoughts of these curiously assorted pilgrims; and the colonel, after some attempts to bring the matter home to himself and the others, was obliged to abandon Mr. Arbuton to his tender reveries of Kitty, and Kitty to her puzzling over the change in Mr. Arbuton. His complaisance made her uncomfortable and shy of him, it was so strange; it gave her a little shiver, as if he were behaving undignifiedly.

"Well, Kitty," said the colonel, "I reckon Uncle Jack would have made more out of this than we've done. He'd have had their geology out of these rocks, any way."

IX

MR. ARBUTON'S INFATUATION

Kitty went as usual to Mrs. Ellison's room after her walk, but she lapsed into a deep abstraction as she sat down beside the sofa.

"What are you smiling at?" asked Mrs. Ellison, after briefly supporting her abstraction.

"Was I smiling?" asked Kitty, beginning to laugh. "I didn't know it."

"What *has* happened so very funny?"

"Why, I don't know whether it's so very funny or not. I believe it isn't funny at all."

"Then what makes you laugh?"

"I don't know. Was I—"

"Now *don't* ask me if you were laughing, Kitty. It's a little too much. You can talk or not, as you choose; but I don't like to be turned into ridicule."

"O Fanny, how can you? I was thinking about something very different. But I don't see how I can tell you, without putting Mr. Arbuton in a ludicrous light, and it isn't quite fair."

W. D. Howells

"You're very careful of him, all at once," said Mrs. Ellison. "You didn't seem disposed to spare him yesterday so much. I don't understand this sudden conversion."

Kitty responded with a fit of outrageous laughter. "Now I see I must tell you," she said, and rapidly recounted Mr. Arbuton's adventure.

"Why, I never knew anything so cool and brave, Fanny, and I admired him more than ever I did; but then I couldn't help seeing the other side of it, you know."

"What other side? I *don't* know."

"Well, you'd have had to laugh yourself, if you'd seen the lordly way he dismissed the poor people who had come running out of their houses to help him, and his stateliness in rewarding that little cooper, and his heroic parting from his cherished overcoat,—which of course he can't replace in Quebec,—and his absent-minded politeness in taking my hand under his arm, and marching off with me so magnificently. But the worst thing, Fanny,"—and she bowed herself under a tempest of long-pent mirth,—"the worst thing was, that the iron, you know, was the cooper's branding-iron, and I had a vision of the dog carrying about on his nose, as long as he lived, the monogram that marks the cooper's casks as holding a certain number of gallons—"

"Kitty, don't be—sacrilegious!" cried Mrs. Ellison.

"No, I'm not," she retorted, gasping and panting. "I never respected Mr. Arbuton so much, and you say yourself I haven't shown myself so careful of him before. But I never was so glad to see Dick in my life, and to have some excuse for laughing. I didn't dare to speak to Mr. Arbuton about it, for he couldn't, if he had tried, have let me laugh it out and be done with it. I trudged demurely along by his side, and neither of us mentioned the matter to Dick," she concluded breathlessly. Then, "I don't know why I should tell you now; it seems wicked and cruel," she said penitently, almost pensively.

Mrs. Ellison had not been amused. She said, "Well, Kitty, in *some* girls I should say it was quite heartless to do as you've done."

"It's heartless in *me*, Fanny; and you needn't say such a thing. I'm sure I didn't utter a syllable to wound him, and just before that he'd been *very* disagreeable, and I forgave him because I thought he was mortified. And you needn't say that I've no feeling"; and thereupon she rose, and, putting her hands into her cousin's, "Fanny," she cried, vehemently, "I *have* been heartless. I'm afraid I haven't shown any sympathy or consideration. I'm afraid I must have seemed dreadfully callous and hard. I oughtn't to have thought of anything but the danger to him; and it seems to me now I scarcely thought of that at all. O, how rude it was of me to see anything funny in it! What *can* I do?"

"Don't go crazy, at any rate, Kitty. *He* doesn't know that you've been laughing about him. You needn't do anything."

"O yes, I need. He doesn't know that I've been laughing about him to you; but, don't you see, I laughed when we met Dick; and what can he think of that?"

"He just thinks you were nervous, I suppose."

"O, do you suppose he does, Fanny? O, I *wish* I could believe that! O, I'm so horribly ashamed of myself! And here yesterday I was criticising him for being unfeeling, and now I've been a thousand times worse than he has ever been, or ever could be! O dear, dear, dear!"

"Kitty! hush!" exclaimed Mrs. Ellison; "you run on like a wild thing, and you're driving me distracted, by not being like yourself."

"O, it's very well for *you* to be so calm; but if you didn't know

W. D. Howells

what to do, you wouldn't."

"Yes, I would; I don't, and I am."

"But what shall I do?" And Kitty plucked away the hands which Fanny had been holding and wrung them. "I'll tell you what I can do," she suddenly added, while a gleam of relief dawned upon her face: "I can bear all his disagreeable ways after this, as long as he stays, and not say anything back. Yes, I'll put up with everything. I'll be as *meek*! He may patronize me and snub me and put me in the wrong as much as he pleases. And then he won't be *approaching* my behavior. O Fanny!"

Upon this, Mrs. Ellison said that she was going to give her a good scolding for her nonsense, and pulled her down and kissed her, and said that she had not done anything, and was, nevertheless, consoled at her resolve to expiate her offence by respecting thenceforward Mr. Arbuton's foibles and prejudices.

It is not certain how far Kitty would have succeeded in her good purposes: these things, so easily conceived, are not of such facile execution; she passed a sleepless night of good resolutions and schemes of reparation; but, fortunately for her, Mr. Arbuton's foibles and prejudices seemed to have fallen into a strange abeyance. The change that had come upon him that day remained; he was still Mr. Arbuton, but with a difference. He could not undo his whole inherited and educated being, and perhaps no chance could deeply affect it without destroying the man. He continued hopelessly superior to Colonel and Mrs. Ellison; but it is not easy to love a woman and not seek, at least before marriage, to please those dear to her. Mr. Arbuton had contested his passion at every advance; he had firmly set his face against the fancy that, at the beginning, invested this girl with a charm; he had only done the things afterwards that mere civilization required; he had suffered torments of doubt concerning her fitness for himself and his place in society; he was not sure yet that her unknown relations were not horribly vulgar people; even yet, he was almost wholly ignorant of the circumstances and conditions of her life. But how he saw her only in the enrapturing light of his daring for her sake, of a self-devotion that had seemed to make her his own; and he behaved toward her with a lover's self-forgetfulness,—or something like it: say a perfect tolerance, a tender patience, in which it would have been hard to detect the lurking shadow of condescension.

He was fairly domesticated with the family. Mrs. Ellison's hurt, in spite of her many imprudences, was decidedly better, and sometimes she made a ceremony of being helped down from her room to dinner; but she always had tea beside her sofa, and he with the others drank it there. Few hours of the day passed in which they did not meet in that easy relation which establishes itself among people sojourning in summer idleness under the same roof. In the morning he saw the young girl fresh and glad as any flower of the garden beneath her window, while the sweet abstraction of her maiden dreams yet hovered in her eyes. At night he sat with her beside the lamp whose light, illuming a little world within, shut out the great world outside, and seemed to be the soft effulgence of her presence, as she sewed, or knit, or read,—a heavenly spirit of home. Sometimes he heard her talking with her cousin, or lightly laughing after he had said good night; once, when he woke, she seemed to be looking out of her window across the moonlight in the Ursulines' Garden while she sang a fragment of song. To meet her on the stairs or in the narrow entries; or to encounter her at the doors, and make way for her to pass with a jest and blush and flutter; to sit down at table with her three times a day,—was a potent witchery. There was a rapture in her shawl flung over the back of a chair; her gloves, lying light as fallen leaves on the table, and keeping the shape of her hands, were full of winning character; and all the more unaccountably they touched his heart because they had a certain careless, sweet shabbiness about the finger-tips.

He found himself hanging upon her desultory talk with Fanny about the set of things and the agreement of colors. There was always more or less of this talk going on, whatever the main topic was, for continual question arose in the minds of one or other lady concerning those adaptations of Mrs. Ellison's finery to the exigencies of Kitty's daily life. They pleased their innocent hearts with the secrecy of the affair, which, in the concealments it required, the sudden difficulties it presented, and the guiltless equivocations it inspired, had the excitement of intrigue. Nothing could have been more to the mind of Mrs. Ellison than to deck Kitty for this perpetual masquerade; and, since the things were very pretty, and Kitty was a girl in every motion of her being, I do not see how anything could have delighted her more than to wear them. Their talk effervesced with the delicious consciousness that he could not dream of what was going on, and babbled over with mysterious jests and laughter, which sometimes he feared to be at his expense, and so joined in, and made them laugh the more at his misconception. He went and came among them at will; he had but to tap at Mrs. Ellison's door, and some voice of unaffected cordiality welcomed him in; he had but to ask, and Kitty was frankly ready for any of those strolls about Quebec in which most of their waking hours were dreamed away.

The gray Lady of the North cast her spell about them,—the freshness of her mornings, the still heat of her middays, the slant, pensive radiance of her afternoons, and the pale splendor of her auroral nights. Never was city so faithfully explored; never did city so abound in objects of interest; for Kitty's love of the place was boundless, and his love for her was inevitable friendship with this adoptive patriotism.

"I didn't suppose you Western people cared for these things," he once said; "I thought your minds were set on things new and square."

"But how could you think so?" replied Kitty, tolerantly. "It's because we have so many new and square things that we like the old crooked ones. I do believe I should enjoy Europe even better than you. There's a forsaken farm-house near Eriecreek, dropping to pieces amongst its wild-grown sweetbriers and quince-bushes, that I used to think a wonder of antiquity because it was built in 1815. Can't you imagine how I must feel in a city like this, that was founded nearly three centuries ago, and has suffered so many sieges and captures, and looks like pictures of those beautiful old towns I can never see?"

"O, perhaps you will see them some day!" he said, touched by her fervor.

"I don't ask it at present: Quebec's enough. I'm in love with the place. I wish I never had to leave it. There isn't a crook, or a turn, or a tin-roof, or a dormer-window, or a gray stone in it that isn't precious."

Mr. Arbuton laughed. "Well, you shall be sovereign lady of Quebec for me. Shall we have the English garrison turned out?"

"No; not unless you can bring back Montcalm's men to take their places."

This might be as they sauntered out of one of the city gates, and strayed through the Lower Town till they should chance upon some poor, bare-interiored church, with a few humble worshippers adoring their Saint, with his lamps alight before his picture; or as they passed some high convent-wall, and caught the strange, metallic clang of the nuns' voices singing their hymns within. Sometimes they whiled away the hours on the Esplanade, breathing its pensive sentiment of neglect and incipient decay, and pacing up and down over the turf athwart the slim shadows of the poplars; or, with comfortable indifference to the local observances, sat in talk on the carriage of one of the burly, uncared-for guns, while the spider wove his web across the mortar's mouth, and the grass nodded above the tumbled pyramids of shot, and the children raced up and down, and the nursery-maids were wooed of the dapper sergeants, and the red-coated sentry loitered lazily to and fro before his box. On the days of the music, they listened to the band in the Governor's Garden, and watched the fine world of the old capital in flirtation with the blond-whiskered officers;

W. D. Howells

and on pleasant nights they mingled with the citizen throng that filled the Durham Terrace, while the river shaped itself in the lights of its shipping, and the Lower Town, with its lamps, lay, like a nether firmament, two hundred feet below them, and Point Levis glittered and sparkled on the thither shore, and in the northern sky the aurora throbbed in swift pulsations of violet and crimson. They liked to climb the Break-Neck Steps at Prescott Gate, dropping from the Upper to the Lower Town, which reminded Mr. Arbuton of Naples and Trieste, and took Kitty with the unassociated picturesqueness of their odd shops and taverns, and their lofty windows green with house-plants. They would stop and look up at the geraniums and fuchsias, and fall a thinking of far different things, and the friendly, unbusy people would come to their doors and look up with them. They recognized the handsome, blond young man, and the pretty, gray-eyed girl; for people in Quebec have time to note strangers who linger there, and Kitty and Mr. Arbuton had come to be well-known figures, different from the fleeting tourists on their rounds; and, indeed, as sojourners they themselves perceived their poetic distinction from mere birds of passage.

Indoors they resorted much to the little entry-window looking out on the Ursulines' Garden. Two chairs stood confronted there, and it was hard for either of the young people to pass them without sinking a moment into one of them, and this appeared always to charm another presence into the opposite chair. There they often lingered in the soft forenoons, talking in desultory phrase of things far and near, or watching, in long silences, the nuns pacing up and down in the garden below, and waiting for the pensive, slender nun, and the stout, jolly nun whom Kitty had adopted, and whom she had gayly interpreted to him as an allegory of Life in their quaint inseparableness; and they played that the influence of one or other nun was in the ascendant, according as their own talk was gay or sad. In their relation, people are not so different from children; they like the same thing over and over again; they like it the better the less it is in itself.

At times Kitty would come with a book in her hand (one finger shut in to keep the place),—some latest novel, or a pirated edition of Longfellow, recreantly purchased at a Quebec bookstore; and then Mr. Arbuton must ask to see it; and he read romance or poetry to her by the hour. He showed to as much advantage as most men do in the serious follies of wooing; and an influence which he could not defy, or would not, shaped him to all the sweet, absurd demands of the affair. From time to time, recollecting himself, and trying to look consequences in the face, he gently turned the talk upon Eriecreek, and endeavored to possess himself of some intelligible image of the place, and of Kitty's home and friends. Even then, the present was so fair and full of content, that his thoughts, when they reverted to the future, no longer met the obstacles that had made him recoil from it before. Whatever her past had been, he could find some way to weaken the ties that bound her to it; a year or two of Europe would leave no trace of Eriecreek; without effort of his, her life would adapt itself to his own, and cease to be a part of the lives of those people there; again and again his amiable imaginations—they were scarcely intents—accomplished themselves in many a swift, fugitive revery, while the days went by, and the shadow of the ivy in the window at which they sat fell, in moonlight and sunlight, upon Kitty's cheeks, and the fuchsia kissed her hair with its purple and crimson blossom.

X

MR. ARBUTON SPEAKS

Mrs. Ellison was almost well; she had already been shopping twice in the Rue Fabrique, and her recovery was now chiefly retarded by the dress-maker's delays in making up a silk too precious to be risked in the piece with the customs officers, at the frontier. Moreover, although the colonel was beginning to chafe, she was not loath to linger yet a few days for the sake of an affair to which her suffering had been a willing sacrifice. In return for her indefatigable self-devotion, Kitty had lately done very little. She ungratefully shrunk more and more from those confidences to which her cousin's speeches covertly invited; she openly resisted open attempts upon her knowledge of facts. If she was not prepared to confess everything to Fanny, it was perhaps because it was all so very little, or because a young girl has not, or ought not to have, a mind in certain matters, or else knows it not, till it is asked her by the one first authorized to learn it. The dream in which she lived was flattering and fair; and it wholly contented her imagination while it lulled her consciousness. It moved from phase to phase without the harshness of reality, and was apparently allied neither to the future nor to the past. She herself seemed to have no more fixity or responsibility in it than the heroine of a romance.

As their last week in Quebec drew to its close, only two or three things remained for them to do, as tourists; and chief among the few unvisited shrines of sentiment was the site of the old Jesuit mission at Sillery.

"It won't do not to see that, Kitty," said Mrs. Ellison, who, as usual, had arranged the details of the excursion, and now announced them. "It's one of the principal things here, and your Uncle Jack would never be satisfied if you missed it. In fact, it's a shame to have left it so long. I can't go with you, for I'm saving up my strength for our picnic at Chateau-Bigot to-morrow; and I want you, Kitty, to see that the colonel sees everything. I've had trouble enough, goodness knows, getting the facts together for him." This was as Kitty and Mr. Arbuton sat waiting in Mrs. Ellison's parlor for the delinquent colonel, who had just stepped round to the Hotel St. Louis and was to be back presently. But the moment of his return passed; a quarter-hour of grace; a half-hour of grim magnanimity,—and still no colonel. Mrs. Ellison began by saying that it was perfectly abominable, and left herself, in a greater extremity, with nothing more forcible to add than that it was too provoking. "It's getting so late now," she said at last, "that it's no use waiting any longer, if you mean to go at all, to-day; and to-day's the only day you *can* go. There, you'd better drive on without him. I can't bear to have you miss it." And, thus adjured, the younger people rose and went.

When the high-born Noel Brulart de Sillery, Knight of Malta and courtier of Marie de Medicis, turned from the vanities of this world and became a priest, Canada was the fashionable mission of the day, and the noble neophyte signalized his self-renunciation by giving of his great wealth for the conversion of the Indian heathen. He supplied the Jesuits with money to maintain a religious establishment near Quebec; and the settlement of red Christians took his musical name, which the region still keeps. It became famous at once as the first residence of the Jesuits and the nuns of the Hotel Dieu, who wrought and suffered for religion there amidst the terrors of pestilence, Iroquois, and winter. It was the scene of miracles and martyrdoms, and marvels of many kinds, and the centre of the missionary efforts among the Indians. Indeed, few events of the picturesque early history of Quebec left it untouched; and it is worthy to be seen, no less for the wild beauty of the spot than for its heroical memories. About a league from the city, where the irregular wall of rock on which Quebec is built recedes from the river, and a grassy space stretches between the tide and the foot of the woody steep, the old mission and the Indian village once stood; and to this day there yet stands the stalwart frame of the first Jesuit Residence, modernized, of course, and turned to secular uses, but firm as of old, and good for a century to come. All round is a world of lumber, and rafts of vast extent cover the face of the waters in the ample cove,— one of many that indent the shore of the St. Lawrence. A careless village straggles along the roadside and the river's margin; huge lumber-ships are loading for Europe in the stream; a town shines out of the woods on the opposite shore; nothing but a friendly climate is needed to make this one of the most charming scenes the heart could imagine.

Kitty and Mr. Arbuton drove out towards Sillery by the St. Louis Road, and already the jealous foliage that hides the pretty villas and stately places of that aristocratic suburb was tinged in here and there a bough with autumnal crimson or yellow; in the meadows here and there a vine ran red along the grass; the loath choke-cherries were ripening in the fence corners; the air was full of the pensive jargoning of the crickets and grasshoppers, and all the subtle sentiment of the fading summer. Their hearts were open to every dreamy influence of the time; their driver understood hardly any English, and their talk might safely be made up of those harmless egotisms which young people exchange,—those strains of psychological autobiography which mark advancing intimacy and in which they appear to each other the most uncommon persons that ever lived, and their experiences and emotions and ideas are the more surprisingly unique because exactly alike.

It seemed a very short league to Sillery when they left the St. Louis Road, and the driver turned his horses' heads towards the river, down the winding sylvan way that descended to the shore; and they had not so much desire, after all, to explore the site of the old mission. Nevertheless, they got out and visited the little space once occupied by the Jesuit chapel, where its foundations may yet be traced in the grass, and they read the inscription on the monument lately raised by the parish to the memory of the first Jesuit missionary to Canada, who died at Sillery. Then there seemed nothing more to do but admire the mighty rafts and piles of lumber; but their show of interest in the local celebrity had stirred the pride of Sillery, and a little French boy entered the chapel-yard, and gave Kitty a pamphlet history of the place, for which he would not suffer himself to be paid; and a sweet-faced young Englishwoman came out of the house across the way, and hesitatingly asked if they would not like to see the Jesuit Residence. She led them indoors, and showed them how the ancient edifice had been encased by the modern house, and bade them note, from the deep shelving window-seats, that the stone walls were three feet thick. The rooms were low-ceiled and quaintly shaped, but they borrowed a certain grandeur from this massiveness; and it was easy to figure the priests in black and the nuns in gray in those dim chambers, which now a life so different inhabited. Behind the house was a plot of grass, and thence the wooded hill rose steep.

"But come up stairs," said the ardent little hostess to Kitty, when her husband came in, and had civilly welcomed the strangers, "and I'll show you my own room, that's as old as any."

They left the two men below, and mounted to a large room carpeted and furnished in modern taste. "We had to take down the old staircase," she continued, "to get our bedstead up,"—a magnificent structure which she plainly thought well worth the sacrifice; and then she pointed out divers remnants of the ancient building. "It's a queer place to live in; but we're only here for the summer"; and she went on to explain, with a pretty *naivete*, how her husband's business brought him to Sillery from Quebec in that season. They were descending the stairs, Kitty foremost, as she added, "This is my first house-keeping, you know, and of course it would be strange anywhere; but you can't think how funny it is here. I suppose," she said, shyly, but as if her confidences merited some return, while Kitty stepped from the stairway face to face with Mr.

Arbuton, who was about to follow them, with the lady's husband,—"I suppose this is your wedding-journey."

A quick alarm flamed through the young girl, and burned out of her glowing cheeks. This pleasant masquerade of hers must look to others like the most intentional love-making between her and Mr. Arbuton,—no dreams either of them, nor figures in a play, nor characters in a romance; nay, on one spectator, at least, it had shed the soft lustre of a honeymoon. How could it be otherwise? Here on this fatal line of wedding-travel,—so common that she remembered Mrs. March half apologized for making it her first tour after marriage,—how could it happen but that two young people together as they were should be taken for bride and bridegroom? Moreover, and worst of all, he must have heard that fatal speech!

He was pale, if she was flushed, and looked grave, as she fancied; but he passed on up the stairs, and she sat down to wait for his return.

"I used to notice so many couples from the States when we lived in the city," continued the hospitable mistress of the house, "but I don't think they often came out to Sillery. In fact, you're the only pair that's come this summer; and so, when you seemed interested about the mission, I thought you wouldn't mind if I spoke to you, and asked you in to see the house. Most of the Americans stay long enough to visit the citadel, and the Plains of Abraham, and the Falls at Montmorenci, and then they go away. I should think they'd be tired always doing the same things. To be sure, they're always different people."

It was unfair to let her entertainer go on talking for quantity in this way; and Kitty said how glad she was to see the old Residence, and that she should always be grateful to her for asking them in. She did not disabuse her of her error; it cost less to leave it alone; and when Mr. Arbuton reappeared, she took leave of those kind people with a sort of remote enjoyment of the wife's mistakenness concerning herself. Yet, as the young matron and her husband stood beside the carriage repeating their adieux, she would fain have prolonged the parting forever, so much she dreaded to be left alone with Mr. Arbuton. But, left alone with him, her spirits violently rose; and as they drove along under the shadow of the cliff, she descanted in her liveliest strain upon the various interests of the way; she dwelt on the beauty of the wide, still river, with the ships at anchor in it; she praised the lovely sunset-light on the other shore; she commented lightly on the village, through which they passed, with the open doors and the suppers frying on the great stoves set into the partition-walls of each cleanly home; she made him look at the two great stairways that climb the cliff from the lumber-yards to the Plains of Abraham, and the army of laborers, each with his empty dinner-pail in hand, scaling the once difficult heights on their way home to the suburb of St. Roch; she did whatever she could to keep the talk to herself and yet away from herself. Part of the way the village was French and neat and pleasant, then it grovelled with Irish people, and ceased to be a tolerable theme for discourse; and so at last the silence against which she had battled fell upon them and deepened like a spell that she could not break.

It would have been better for Mr. Arbuton's success just then if he had not broken it. But failure was not within his reckoning; for he had so long regarded this young girl *de haut en bas*, to say it brutally, that he could not imagine she should feel any doubt in accepting him. Moreover, a magnanimous sense of obligation mingled with his confident love, for she must have known that he had overheard that speech at the Residence. Perhaps he let this feeling color his manner, however faintly. He lacked the last fine instinct; he could not forbear; and he spoke while all her nerves and fluttering pulses cried him mercy.

XI

KITTY ANSWERS

It was dimmest twilight when Kitty entered Mrs. Ellison's room and sank down on the first chair in silence.

"The colonel met a friend at the St. Louis, and forgot about the expedition, Kitty," said Fanny, "and he only came in half an hour ago. But it's just as well; I know you've had a splendid time. Where's Mr. Arbuton?"

Kitty burst into tears.

"Why, has anything happened to him?" cried Mrs. Ellison, springing towards her.

"To him? No! What should happen to *him*?" Kitty demanded with an indignant accent.

"Well, then, has anything happened to *you*?"

"I don't know if you can call it *happening*. But I suppose you'll be satisfied now, Fanny. He's offered himself to me." Kitty uttered the last words with a sort of violence, as if since the fact must be stated, she wished it to appear in the sharpest relief.

"O dear!" said Mrs. Ellison, not so well satisfied as the success-ful match-maker ought to be. So long as it was a marriage in the abstract, she had never ceased to desire it; but as the actual union of Kitty and this Mr. Arbuton, of whom, really, they knew so little, and of whom, if she searched her heart, she had as little liking as knowledge, it was another affair. Mrs. Ellison trembled at her triumph, and began to think that failure would have been easier to bear. Were they in the least suited to each other? Would she like to see poor Kitty chained for life to that impassive egotist, whose very merits were repellent, and whose modesty even seemed to convict and snub you? Mrs. Ellison was not able to put the matter to herself with moderation, either way; doubtless she did Mr. Arbuton injustice now. "Did you accept him?" she whispered, feebly.

"Accept him?" repeated Kitty. "No!"

"O dear!" again sighed Mrs. Ellison, feeling that this was scarcely better, and not daring to ask further.

"I'm dreadfully perplexed, Fanny," said Kitty, after waiting for the questions which did not come, "and I wish you'd help me think."

"I will, darling. But I don't know that I'll be of much use. I begin to think I'm not very good at thinking."

Kitty, who longed chiefly to get the situation more distinctly before herself, gave no heed to this confession, but went on to rehearse the whole affair. The twilight lent her its veil; and in the kindly obscurity she gathered courage to face all the facts, and even to find what was droll in them.

"It was very solemn, of course, and I was frightened; but I tried to keep my wits about me, and *not* to say yes, simply because that was the easiest thing. I told him that I didn't know,—and I don't; and that I must have time to think,—and I must. He was very ungenerous, and said he had hoped I had already had time to think; and he couldn't seem to understand, or else I couldn't very well explain, how it had been with me all along."

"He might certainly say you had encouraged him," Mrs.

Ellison remarked, thoughtfully.

"Encouraged him, Fanny? How can you accuse me of such indelicacy?"

"Encouraging isn't indelicacy. The gentlemen *have* to be encouraged, or of course they'd never have any courage. They're so timid, naturally."

"I don't think Mr. Arbuton is very timid. He seemed to think that he had only to ask as a matter of form, and I had no business to say anything. What has he ever done for me? And hasn't he often been intensely disagreeable? He oughtn't to have spoken just after overhearing what he did. It was horrid to do so. He was very obtuse, too, not to see that girls can't always be so certain of themselves as men, or, if they are, don't know they are as soon as they're asked."

"Yes," interrupted Mrs. Ellison, "that's the way with girls. I do believe that most of them—when they're young like you, Kitty—never think of marriage as the end of their flirtations. They'd just like the attentions and the romance to go on forever, and never turn into anything more serious; and they're not to blame for that, though they *do* get blamed for it."

"Certainly," assented Kitty, eagerly, "that's it; that's just what I was saying; that's the very reason why girls must have time to make up their minds. *You* had, I suppose."

"Yes, two minutes. Poor Dick was going back to his regiment, and stood with his watch in his hand. I said no, and called after him to correct myself. But, Kitty, if the romance had happened to stop without his saying anything, you wouldn't have liked that either, would you?"

"No," faltered Kitty, "I suppose not."

"Well, then, don't you see? That's a great point in his favor. How much time did you want, or did he give you?"

"I said I should answer before we left Quebec," answered Kitty, with a heavy sigh.

"Don't you know what to say now?"

"I can't tell. That's what I want you to help me think out."

Mrs. Ellison was silent for a moment before she said, "Well, then, I suppose we shall have to go back to the very beginning."

"Yes," assented Kitty, faintly.

"You did have a sort of fancy for him the first time you saw him, didn't you?" asked Mrs. Ellison, coaxingly, while forcing herself to be systematic and coherent, by a mental strain of which no idea can be given.

"Yes," said Kitty, yet more faintly, adding, "but I can't tell just what sort of a fancy it was. I suppose I admired him for being handsome and stylish, and for having such exquisite manners."

"Go on," said Mrs. Ellison. "And after you got acquainted with him?"

"Why, you know we've talked that over once already, Fanny."

"Yes, but we oughtn't to skip anything now," replied Mrs. Ellison, in a tone of judicial accuracy which made Kitty smile.

But she quickly became serious again, and said, "Afterwards I couldn't tell whether to like him or not, or whether he wanted me to. I think he acted very strangely for a person in—love. I used to feel so troubled and oppressed when I was with him. He seemed always to be making himself agreeable under protest."

"Perhaps that was just your imagination, Kitty."

"Perhaps it was; but it troubled me just the same."

"Well, and then?"

"Well, and then after that day of the Montgomery expedition, he seemed to change altogether, and to try always to be pleasant, and to do everything he could to make me like him. I don't know how to account for it. Ever since then he's been extremely careful of me, and behaved—of course without knowing it—as if I belonged to him already. Or maybe I've imagined that too. It's very hard to tell what has really happened the last two weeks."

Kitty was silent, and Mrs. Ellison did not speak at once. Presently she asked, "Was his acting as if you belonged to him disagreeable?"

"I can't tell. I think it was rather presuming. I don't know why he did it."

"Do you respect him?" demanded Mrs. Ellison.

"Why, Fanny, I've always told you that I did respect some things in him."

Mrs. Ellison had the facts before her, and it rested upon her to sum them up, and do something with them. She rose to a sitting posture, and confronted her task.

"Well, Kitty, I'll tell you: I don't really know what to think. But I can say this: if you liked him at first, and then didn't like him, and afterwards he made himself more agreeable, and you didn't mind his behaving as if you belonged to him, and you respected him, but after all didn't think him fascinating—"

"He *is* fascinating—in a kind of way. He was, from the beginning. In a story his cold, snubbing, putting-down ways would have been perfectly fascinating."

"Then why didn't you take him?"

"Because," answered Kitty, between laughing and crying, "it isn't a story, and I don't know whether I like him."

"But do you think you might get to like him?"

"I don't know. His asking brings back all the doubts I ever had of him, and that I've been forgetting the past two weeks. I can't tell whether I like him or not. If I did, shouldn't I trust him more?"

"Well, whether you are in love or not, I'll tell you what you *are*, Kitty," cried Mrs. Ellison, provoked with her indecision, and yet relieved that the worst, whatever it was, was postponed thereby for a day or two.

"What!"

"You're—"

But at this important juncture the colonel came lounging in, and Kitty glided out of the room.

"Richard," said Mrs. Ellison, seriously, and in a tone implying that it was the colonel's fault, as usual, "you know what has happened, I suppose."

"No, my dear, I don't; but no matter: I will presently, I dare say."

"O, I wish for once you wouldn't be so flippant. Mr. Arbuton has offered himself to Kitty."

Colonel Ellison gave a quick, sharp whistle of amazement, but trusted himself to nothing more articulate.

"Yes," said his wife, responding to the whistle, "and it makes me perfectly wretched."

"Why, I thought you liked him."

"I didn't *like* him; but I thought it would be an excellent thing for Kitty."

"And won't it?"

"She doesn't know."

"Doesn't know?"

"No."

The colonel was silent, while Mrs. Ellison stated the case in full, and its pending uncertainty. Then he exclaimed vehemently, as if his amazement had been growing upon him, "This is the most astonishing thing in the world! Who would ever have dreamt of that young iceberg being in love?"

"Haven't I *told* you all along he was?"

"O yes, certainly; but that might be taken either way, you know. You would discover the tender passion in the eye of a potato."

"Colonel Ellison," said Fanny with sternness, "why do you suppose he's been hanging about us for the last four weeks? Why should he have stayed in Quebec? Do you think he pitied *me*, or found *you* so very agreeable?"

"Well, I thought he found us just tolerable, and was interested in the place."

Mrs. Ellison made no direct reply to this pitiable speech, but looked a scorn which, happily for the colonel, the darkness hid. Presently she said that bats did not express the blindness of men, for any bat could have seen what was going on.

"Why," remarked the colonel, "I did have a momentary

suspicion that day of the Montgomery business; they both looked very confused, when I saw them at the end of that street, and neither of them had anything to say; but that was accounted for by what you told me afterwards about his adventure. At the time I didn't pay much attention to the matter. The idea of his being in love seemed too ridiculous."

"Was it ridiculous for you to be in love with me?"

"No; and yet I can't praise my condition for its wisdom, Fanny."

"Yes! that's *like* men. As soon as one of them is safely married, he thinks all the love-making in the world has been done forever, and he can't conceive of two young people taking a fancy to each other."

"That's something so, Fanny. But granting—for the sake of argument merely—that Boston has been asking Kitty to marry him, and she doesn't know whether she wants him, what are we to do about it? *I* don't like him well enough to plead his cause; do you? When does Kitty think she'll be able to make up her mind?"

"She's to let him know before we leave."

The colonel laughed. "And so he's to hang about here on uncertainties for two whole days! That *is* rather rough on him. Fanny, what made you so eager for this business?"

"Eager? I *wasn't* eager."

"Well, then,—reluctantly acquiescent?"

"Why, she's so literary and that."

"And what?"

"How insulting!—Intellectual, and so on; and I thought she

would be just fit to live in a place where everybody is literary and intellectual. That is, I thought that, if I thought anything."

"Well," said the colonel, "you may have been right on the whole, but I don't think Kitty is showing any particular force of mind, just now, that would fit her to live in Boston. My opinion is, that it's ridiculous for her to keep him in suspense. She might as well answer him first as last. She's putting herself under a kind of obligation by her delay. I'll talk to her—"

"If you do, you'll kill her. You don't know how she's wrought up about it."

"O well, I'll be careful of her sensibilities. It's my duty to speak with her. I'm here in the place of a parent. Besides, don't I know Kitty? I've almost brought her up."

"Maybe you're right. You're all so queer that perhaps you're right. Only, do be careful, Richard. You must approach the matter very delicately,—indirectly, you know. Girls are different, remember, from young men, and you mustn't be blunt. Do maneuver a little, for once in your life."

"All right, Fanny; you needn't be afraid of my doing anything awkward or sudden. I'll go to her room pretty soon, after she is quieted down, and have a good, calm old fatherly conversation with her."

The colonel was spared this errand; for Kitty had left some of her things on Fanny's table, and now came back for them with a lamp in her hand. Her averted face showed the marks of weeping; the corners of her firm-set lips were downward bent, as if some resolution which she had taken were very painful. This the anxious Fanny saw; and she made a gesture to the colonel which any woman would have understood to enjoin silence, or, at least, the utmost caution and tenderness of speech. The colonel summoned his *finesse* and said, cheerily, "Well, Kitty, what's Boston been saying to you?"

Mrs. Ellison fell back upon her sofa as if shot, and placed her hand over her face.

Kitty seemed not to hear her cousin. Having gathered up her things, she bent an unmoved face and an unseeing gaze full upon him, and glided from the room without a word.

"Well, upon my soul," cried the colonel, "this is a pleasant, nightmarish, sleep-walking, Lady-Macbethish little transaction. Confound it, Fanny this comes of your wanting me to maneuver. If you'd let me come straight *at* the subject,—like a *man*—"

"*Please*, Richard, don't say anything more now," pleaded Mrs. Ellison in a broken voice. "You can't help it, I know; and I must do the best I can, under the circumstances. Do go away for a little while, darling! O dear!"

As for Kitty, when she had got out of the room in that phantasmal fashion, she dimly recalled, through the mists of her own trouble, the colonel's dismay at her so glooming upon him, and began to think that she had used poor Dick more tragically than she need, and so began to laugh softly to herself; but while she stood there at the entry window a moment, laughing in the moonlight, that made her lamp-flame thin, and painted her face with its pale lustre, Mr. Arbuton came down the attic stairway. He was not a man of quick fancies; but to one of even slower imagination and of calmer mood, she might very well have seemed unreal, the creature of a dream, fantastic, intangible, insensible, arch, not wholly without some touch of the malign. In his heart he groaned over her beauty as if she were lost to him forever in this elfish transfiguration.

"Miss Ellison!" he scarcely more than whispered.

"You ought not to speak to me now," she answered, gravely.

"I know it; but I could not help it. For heaven's sake, do not let it tell against me. I wished to ask if I should not see you to-morrow; to beg that all might go on as had been planned, and as if nothing had been said to-day."

"It'll be very strange," said Kitty. "My cousins know everything now. How can we meet before them!"

"I'm not going away without an answer, and we can't remain here without meeting. It will be less strange if we let everything take its course."

"Well."

"Thanks."

He looked strangely humbled, but even more bewildered than humbled.

She listened while he descended the steps, unbolted the street door, and closed it behind him. Then she passed out of the moonlight into her own room, whose close-curtained space the lamp filled with its ruddy glow, and revealed her again, no malicious sprite, but a very puzzled, conscientious, anxious young girl.

Of one thing, at least, she was clear. It had all come about through misunderstanding, through his taking her to be something that she was not; for she was certain that Mr. Arbuton was of too worldly a spirit to choose, if he had known, a girl of such origin and lot as she was only too proud to own. The deception must have begun with dress; and she determined that her first stroke for truth and sincerity should be most sublimely made in the return of Fanny's things, and a rigid fidelity to her own dresses. "Besides," she could not help reflecting, "my travelling-suit will be just the thing for a picnic." And here, if the cynical reader of another sex is disposed to sneer at the method of her self-devotion, I am sure that women, at least, will allow it was most natural and highly proper that in this great moment she should first think of dress, upon which so great consequences hang in matters of the heart Who—to be honest for once, O vain and conceited men!—can deny that the cut, the color, the texture, the stylish set of dresses, has not had everything to do with the rapture of love's young dream? Are not certain bits of lace and knots of ribbon as much a part of it as any smile or sidelong glance of them all? And hath not the long experience of the fair taught them that artful dress is half the virtue of their spells? Full well they know it; and when Kitty resolved to profit no longer by Fanny's wardrobe, she had won the hardest part of the battle in behalf of perfect truth towards Mr. Arbuton. She did not, indeed, stop with this, but lay awake, devising schemes by which she should disabuse him of his errors about her, and persuade him that she was no wife for him.

W. D. Howells

XII

THE PICNIC AT CHATEAU-BIGOT

"Well," said Mrs. Ellison, who had slipped into Kitty's room, in the morning, to do her back hair with some advantages of light which her own chamber lacked, "it'll be no crazier than the rest of the performance; and if you and he can stand it, I'm sure that *we*'ve no reason to complain."

"Why, I don't see how it's to be helped, Fanny. He's asked it; and I'm rather glad he has, for I should have hated to have the conventional headache that keeps young ladies from being seen; and at any rate I don't understand how the day could be passed more sensibly than just as we originally planned to spend it. I can make up my mind a great deal better with him than away from him. But I think there never was a more ridiculous situation: now that the high tragedy has faded out of it, and the serious part is coming, it makes me laugh. Poor Mr. Arbuton will feel all day that he is under my mercilessly critical eye, and that he mustn't do this and he mustn't say that, for fear of me; and he can't run away, for he's promised to wait patiently for my decision. It's a most inglorious position for him, but I don't think of anything to do about it. I could say no at once, but he'd rather not."

"What have you got that dress on for?" asked Mrs. Ellison, abruptly.

"Because I'm not going to wear your things any more, Fanny.

It's a case of conscience. I feel like a guilty creature, being courted in another's clothes; and I don't know but it's for a kind of punishment of my deceit that I can't realize this affair as I ought, or my part in it. I keep feeling, the whole time, as if it were somebody else, and I have an absurd kind of other person's interest in it."

Mrs. Ellison essayed some reply, but was met by Kitty's steadfast resolution, and in the end did not prevail in so much as a ribbon for her hair.

It was not till well into the forenoon that the preparations for the picnic were complete and the four set off together in one carriage. In the strong need that was on each of them to make the best of the affair, the colonel's unconsciousness might have been a little overdone, but Mrs. Ellison's demeanor was sublimely successful. The situation gave full play to her peculiar genius, and you could not have said that any act of hers failed to contribute to the perfection of her design, that any tone or speech was too highly colored. Mr. Arbuton, of whom she took possession, and who knew that she knew all, felt that he had never done justice to her, and seconded her efforts with something like cordial admiration; while Kitty, with certain grateful looks and aversions of the face, paid an ardent homage to her strokes of tact, and after a few miserable moments, in which her nightlong trouble gnawed at her heart, began, in spite of herself, to enjoy the humor of the situation.

It is a lovely road out to Chateau-Bigot. First you drive through the ancient suburbs of the Lower Town, and then you mount the smooth, hard highway, between pretty country-houses, toward the village of Charlesbourg, while Quebec shows, to your casual backward-glance, like a wondrous painted scene, with the spires and lofty roofs of the Upper Town, and the long, irregular wall wandering on the verge of the cliff; then the thronging gables and chimneys of St. Roch, and again many spires and convent walls; lastly the shipping in the St. Charles, which, in one direction, runs, a narrowing gleam, up into its valley, and in the other widens into the broad light of the St. Lawrence. Quiet, elmy spaces of meadow land stretch between the suburban mansions and the village of Charlesbourg, where the driver reassured himself as to his route from the group of idlers on the platform before the church. Then he struck off on a country road, and presently turned from this again into a lane that grew rougher and rougher, till at last it lapsed to a mere cart-track among the woods, where the rich, strong odors of the pine, and of the wild herbs bruised under the wheels, filled the air. A peasant and his black-eyed, open-mouthed boy were cutting withes to bind hay at the side of the track, and the latter consented to show the strangers to the chateau from a point beyond which they could not go with the carriage. There the small habitant and the driver took up the picnic-baskets, and led the way through pathless growths of underbrush to a stream, so swift that it is said never to freeze, so deeply sprung that the summer never drinks it dry. A screen of water-growths bordered it; and when this was passed, a wide open space revealed itself, with the ruin of the chateau in the midst.

The pathos of long neglect lay upon the scene; for here were evidences of gardens and bowery aisles in other times, and now, for many a year, desolation and the slow return of the wilderness. The mountain rising behind the chateau grounds showed the dying flush of the deciduous leaves among the dark green of the pines that clothed it to the crest; a cry of innumerable crickets filled the ear of the dreaming noon.

The ruin itself is not of impressive size, and it is a chateau by grace of the popular fancy rather than through any right of its own; for it was, in truth, never more than the hunting-lodge of the king's Intendant, Bigot, a man whose sins claim for him a lordly consideration in the history of Quebec, He was the last Intendant before the British conquest, and in that time of general distress he grew rich by oppression of the citizens, and by peculation from the soldiers. He built this pleasure-house here in the woods, and hither he rode out from Quebec to enjoy himself in the chase and the carouses that succeed the chase. Here, too, it is said, dwelt in secret the Huron girl who loved him, and who survives in the memory of the peasants as the murdered *sauragesse*; and, indeed, there is as much proof that she was murdered as that she ever lived. When the wicked Bigot was arrested and sent to France, where he was tried with great result of documentary record, his chateau fell into other hands; at last a party of Arnold's men wintered there in 1775, and it is to our own countrymen that we owe the conflagration and the ruin of Chateau-Bigot. It stands, as I said, in the middle of that open place, with the two gable walls and the stone partition-wall still almost entire, and that day showing very effectively against the tender northern sky. On the most weatherward gable the iron in the stone had shed a dark red stain under the lash of many winter storms, and some tough lichens had incrusted patches of the surface; but, for the rest, the walls rose in the univied nakedness of all ruins in our climate, which has no clinging evergreens wherewith to pity and soften the forlornness of decay. Out of the rubbish at the foot of the walls there sprang a wilding growth of syringas and lilacs; and the interior was choked with flourishing weeds, and with the briers of the raspberry, on which a few berries hung. The heavy beams, left where they fell a hundred years ago, proclaimed the honest solidity with which the chateau had been built, and there was proof in the cut stone of the hearths and chimney-places that it had once had at least the ambition of luxury.

While its visitors stood amidst the ruin, a harmless garden-snake slipped out of one crevice into another; from her nest in some hidden corner overhead a silent bird flew away. For the moment,—so slight is the capacity of any mood, so deeply is the heart responsive to a little impulse,—the palace of the Caesars could not have imparted a keener sense of loss and desolation. They eagerly sought such particulars of the ruin as agreed with the descriptions they had read of it, and were as well contented with a bit of cellar-way outside as if they had really found the secret passage to the subterranean chamber of the chateau, or the hoard of silver which the little habitant said was buried under it. Then they dispersed about the grounds to trace out the borders of the garden, and Mr. Arbuton won the common praise by discovering the foundations of the stable of the chateau.

Then there was no more to do but to prepare for the picnic. They chose a grassy plot in the shadow of a half-dismantled bark-lodge,—a relic of the Indians, who resort to the place every summer. In the ashes of that sylvan hearth they kindled their fire, Mr. Arbuton gathering the sticks, and the colonel showing a peculiar genius in adapting the savage flames to the limitations of the civilized coffee-pot borrowed of Mrs. Gray. Mrs. Ellison laid the cloth, much meditating the arrangement of the viands, and reversing again and again the relative positions of the sliced tongue and the sardines that flanked the cold roast chicken, and doubting dreadfully whether to put down the cake and the canned peaches at once, or reserve them for a second course; the stuffed olives drove her to despair, being in a bottle, and refusing to be balanced by anything less monumental in shape. Some wild asters and red leaves and green and yellowing sprays of fern which Kitty arranged in a tumbler were hailed with rapture, but presently flung far away with fierce disdain because they had ants on them. Kitty witnessed this outburst with her usual complacency, and then went on making the coffee. With such blissful pain as none but lovers know, Mr. Arbuton saw her break the egg upon the edge of the coffee-pot, and let it drop therein, and then, with a charming frenzy, stir it round and round. It was a picture of domestic suggestion, a subtle insinuation of home, the unconscious appeal of inherent housewifery to inherent husband-hood. At the crash of the eggshell he trembled; the swift agitation of the coffee and the egg within the pot made him dizzy.

"Sha'n't I stir that for you, Miss Ellison?" he said, awkwardly.

"O dear, no!" she answered in surprise at a man's presuming to stir coffee; "but you may go get me some water at the creek, if you please."

She gave him a pitcher, and he went off to the brook, which

was but a minute's distance away. This minute, however, left her alone, for the first time that day, with both Dick and Fanny, and a silence fell upon all three at once. They could not help looking at one another; and then the colonel, to show that he was not thinking of anything, began to whistle, and Mrs. Ellison rebuked him for whistling.

"Why not?" he asked. "It isn't a funeral, is it?"

"Of course it isn't," said Mrs. Ellison; and Kitty, who had been blushing to the verge of tears, laughed instead, and then was consumed with vexation when Mr. Arbuton came up, feeling that he must suspect himself the motive of her ill-timed mirth. "The champagne ought to be cooled, I suppose," observed Mrs. Ellison, when the coffee had been finally stirred and set to boil on the coals.

"I'm best acquainted with the brook," said Mr. Arbuton, "and I know just the eddy in it where the champagne will cool soonest."

"Then you shall take it there," answered the governess of the feast; and Mr. Arbuton duteously set off with the bottle in his hand.

The pitcher of water which he had already brought stood in the grass; by a sudden movement of the skirt, Kitty knocked it over. The colonel made a start forward; Mrs. Ellison arrested him with a touch, while she bent a look of ineffable admiration upon Kitty.

"Now, I'll teach myself," said Kitty, "that I can't be so clumsy with impunity. I'll go and fill that pitcher again myself." She hurried after Mr. Arbuton; they scarcely spoke going or coming; but the constraint that Kitty felt was nothing to that she had dreaded in seeking to escape from the tacit raillery of the colonel and the championship of Fanny. Yet she trembled to realize that already her life had become so far entangled with this stranger's, that she found refuge with him from her own kindred. They could do nothing to help her in this; the trouble was solely hers and his, and they two must get out of it one way or other themselves; the case scarcely admitted even of sympathy, and if it had not been hers, it would have been one to amuse her rather than appeal to her compassion. Even as it was, she sometimes caught herself smiling at the predicament of a young girl who had passed a month in every appearance of love-making, and who, being asked her heart, was holding her lover in suspense whilst she searched it, and meantime was picnicking with him upon the terms of casual flirtation. Of all the heroines in her books, she knew none in such a strait as this.

But her perplexities did not impair the appetite which she brought to the sylvan feast. In her whole simple life she had never tasted champagne before, and she said innocently, as she put the frisking fluid from her lips after the first taste, "Why, I thought you had to *learn* to like champagne."

"No," remarked the colonel, "it's like reading and writing: it comes by nature. I suppose that even one of the lower animals would like champagne. The refined instinct of young ladies makes them recognize its merits instantly. Some of the Confederate cellars," added the colonel, thoughtfully, "had very good champagne in them. Green seal was the favorite of our erring brethren. It wasn't one of their errors. I prefer it myself to our own native cider, whether made of apples or grapes. Yes, it's better even than the water from the old chain-pump in the back yard at Eriecreek, though it hasn't so fine a flavor of lubricating oil in it."

The faint chill that touched Mr. Arbuton at the mention of Eriecreek and its petrolic associations was transient. He was very light of heart, since the advance that Kitty seemed to have made him; and in his temporary abandon he talked well, and promoted the pleasure of the time without critical reserves. When the colonel, with the reluctance of our soldiers to speak of their warlike experiences before civilians, had suffered himself to tell a story that his wife begged of him about his last battle, Mr. Arbuton listened with a deference that flattered poor Mrs. Ellison, and made her marvel at Kitty's doubt concerning him; and then he spoke entertainingly of some travel experiences of his own, which he politely excused as quite unworthy to come after the colonel's story. He excused them a little too much, and just gave the modest soldier a faint, uneasy fear of having boasted. But no one else felt this result of his delicacy, and the feast was merry enough. When it was ended, Mrs. Ellison, being still a little infirm of foot, remained in the shadow of the bark-lodge, and the colonel lit his cigar, and loyally stretched himself upon the grass before her.

There was nothing else for Kitty and Mr. Arbuton but to stroll off together, and she preferred to do this.

They sauntered up to the chateau in silence, and peered somewhat languidly about the ruin. On a bit of smooth surface in a sheltered place many names of former visitors were written, and Mr. Arbuton said he supposed they might as well add those of their own party.

"O yes," answered Kitty, with a half-sigh, seating herself upon a fallen stone, and letting her hands fall into each other in her lap as her wont was, "you write them." A curious pensiveness passed from one to the other and possessed them both.

Mr. Arbuton began to write. Suddenly, "Miss Ellison," said he, with a smile, "I've blundered in your name; I neglected to put the Miss before it; and now there isn't room on the plastering."

"O, never mind," replied Kitty, "I dare say it won't be missed!"

Mr. Arbuton neither perceived nor heeded the pun. He was looking in a sort of rapture at the name which his own hand had written now for the first time, and he felt an indecorous desire to kiss it.

"If I could speak it as I've written it—"

"I don't see what harm there would be in that," said the owner of the name, "or what object," she added more discreetly.

—"I should feel that I had made a great gain."

"I never told you," answered Kitty, evasively, "how much I admire *your* first name, Mr. Arbuton."

"How did you know it?"

"It was on the card you gave my cousin," said Kitty, frankly, but thinking he now must know she had been keeping his card.

"It's an old family name,—a sort of heirloom from the first of us who came to the country; and in every generation since, some Arbuton has had to wear it."

"It's superb!" cried Kitty. "Miles! 'Miles Standish, the Puritan captain,' 'Miles Standish, the Captain of Plymouth.' I should be very proud of such a name."

"You have only to take it," he said, gravely.

"O, I didn't mean that," she said with a blush, and then added, "Yours is a very old family, then, isn't it?"

"Yes, it's pretty well," answered Mr. Arbuton, "but it's not such a rare thing in the East, you know."

"I suppose not. The Ellisons are *not* an old family. If we went back of my uncle, we should only come to backwoodsmen and Indian fighters. Perhaps that's the reason we don't care much for old families. You think a great deal of them in Boston, don't you?"

"We do, and we don't. It's a long story, and I'm afraid I couldn't make you understand, unless you had seen something of Boston society."

"Mr. Arbuton," said Kitty, abruptly plunging to the bottom of the subject on which they had been hovering, "I'm dreadfully afraid that what you said to me—what you asked of me, yesterday—was all through a misunderstanding. I'm afraid that you've somehow mistaken me and my circumstances, and that somehow I've innocently helped on your mistake."

"There is no mistake," he answered, eagerly, "about my loving you!"

Kitty did not look up, nor answer this outburst, which flattered while it pained her. She said, "I've been so much mistaken myself, and I've been so long finding it out, that I should feel anxious to have you know just what kind of girl you'd asked to be your wife, before I—"

"What?"

"Nothing. But I should want you to know that in many things my life has been very, very different from yours. The first thing I can remember—you'll think I'm more autobiographical than our driver at Ha-Ha Bay, even, but I must tell you all this—is about Kansas, where we had moved from Illinois, and of our having hardly enough to eat or wear, and of my mother grieving over our privations. At last, when my father was killed," she said, dropping her voice, "in front of our own door—"

Mr. Arbuton gave a start. "Killed?"

"Yes; didn't you know? Or no: how could you? He was shot by the Missourians."

Whether it was not hopelessly out of taste to have a father-in-law who had been shot by the Missourians? Whether he could persuade Kitty to suppress that part of her history? That she looked very pretty, sitting there, with her earnest eyes lifted toward his. These things flashed wilfully through Mr. Arbuton's mind.

"My father was a Free-State man," continued Kitty, in a tone of pride. "He wasn't when he first went to Kansas," she added simply; while Mr. Arbuton groped among his recollections of that forgotten struggle for some association with these names, keenly feeling the squalor of it all, and thinking still how very pretty she was. "He went out there to publish a proslavery paper. But when he found out what the Border Ruffians really were, he turned against them. He used to be very bitter about my uncle's having become an Abolitionist; they had had a quarrel about it; but father wrote to him from Kansas, and they made it up; and before father died he was able to tell mother that we were to go to uncle's. But mother was sick then, and she only lived a month after father; and when my cousin came out to get us, just before she died, there was scarcely a crust of cornbread in our cabin. It seemed like heaven to get to Eriecreek; but even at Eriecreek we live in a way that I am afraid you wouldn't respect. My uncle has just enough, and we are very plain people indeed. I suppose," continued the young girl meekly, "that I haven't had at all what you'd call an education. Uncle told me what to read, at first, and after that I helped myself. It seemed to come naturally; but don't you see that it wasn't an education?"

"I beg pardon," said Mr. Arbuton, with a blush; for he had just then lost the sense of what she said in the music of her voice, as it hesitated over these particulars of her history.

"I mean," explained Kitty, "that I'm afraid I must be very one-sided. I'm dreadfully ignorant of a great many things. I haven't any accomplishments, only the little bit of singing and playing that you've heard; I couldn't tell a good picture from a bad one; I've never been to the opera; I don't know anything about society. Now just imagine," cried Kitty, with sublime impartiality, "such a girl as that in Boston!"

Even Mr. Arbuton could not help smiling at this comic earnestness, while she resumed: "At home my cousins and I do all kinds of things that the ladies whom you know have done for them. We do our own work, for one thing," she continued, with a sudden treacherous misgiving that what she was saying might be silly and not heroic, but bravely stifling her doubt. "My cousin Virginia is housekeeper, and Rachel does the sewing, and I'm a kind of maid-of-all-work."

Mr. Arbuton listened respectfully, vainly striving for some likeness of Miss Ellison in the figure of the different second-girls who, during life, had taken his card, or shown him into drawing-rooms, or waited on him at table; failing in this, he tried her in the character of daughter of that kind of farm-house where they take summer boarders and do their own work; but evidently the Ellisons were not of that sort either; and he gave it up and was silent, not knowing what to say, while Kitty, a little piqued by his silence, went on: "We're not ashamed, you understand, of our ways; there's such a thing as being proud of not being proud; and that's what we are, or what I am; for the rest are not mean enough ever to think about it, and once I wasn't, either. But that's the kind of life I'm used to; and though I've read of other kinds of life a great deal, I've not been brought up to anything different, don't you understand? And maybe—I don't know—I mightn't like or respect your kind of people any more than they did me. My uncle taught us ideas that are quite different from yours; and what if I shouldn't be able to give them up?"

"There is only one thing I know or see: I love you!" he said, passionately, and drew nearer by a step; but she put out her hand and repelled him with a gesture.

"Sometimes you might be ashamed of me before those you knew to be my inferiors,—really common and coarse-minded people, but regularly educated, and used to money and fashion. I should cower before them, and I never could forgive you."

"I've one answer to all this: I love you!"

Kitty flushed in generous admiration of his magnanimity, and said, with more of tenderness than she had yet felt towards

W. D. Howells

him, "I'm sorry that I can't answer you now, as you wish, Mr. Arbuton."

"But you will, to-morrow."

She shook her head. "I don't know; O, I don't know! I've been thinking of something. That Mrs. March asked me to visit her in Boston; but we had given up doing so, because of the long delay here. If I asked my cousins, they'd still go home that way. It's too bad to put you off again; but you must see me in Boston, if only for a day or two, and after you've got back into your old associations there, before I answer you. I'm in great trouble. You must wait, or I must say no."

"I'll wait," said Mr. Arbuton.

"O, *thank* you," sighed Kitty, grateful for this patience, and not for the chance of still winning him; "you are very forbearing, I'm sure."

She again put forth her hand, but not now to repel him. He clasped it, and kept it in his, then impulsively pressed it against his lips.

Colonel and Mrs. Ellison had been watching the whole pantomime, forgotten.

"Well," said the colonel, "I suppose that's the end of the play, isn't it? I don't like it, Fanny; I don't like it."

"Hush!" whispered Mrs. Ellison.

They were both puzzled when Kitty and Mr. Arbuton came towards them with anxious faces. Kitty was painfully revolving in her mind what she had just said, and thinking she had said not so much as she meant and yet so much more, and tormenting herself with the fear that she had been at once too bold and too meek in her demand for longer delay. Did it not give him further claim upon her? Must it not have seemed a very audacious thing? What right had she to make it, and how could she now finally say no? Then the matter of her explanation to him: was it in the least what she meant to say? Must it not give him an idea of intellectual and spiritual poverty in her life which she knew had not been in it? Would he not believe, in spite of her boasts, that she was humiliated before him by a feeling of essential inferiority? O, *had* she boasted? What she meant to do was just to make him understand clearly what she was; but, had she? Could he be made to understand this with what seemed his narrow conception of things outside of his own experience? Was it worth while to try? Did she care enough for him to make the effort desirable? Had she made it for his sake, or in the interest of truth, merely, or in self-defence?

These and a thousand other like questions beset her the whole way home to Quebec, amid the frequent pauses of the talk, and underneath whatever she was saying. Half the time she answered yes or no to them, and not to what Dick, or Fanny, or Mr. Arbuton had asked her; she was distraught with their recurrence, as they teased about her like angry bees, and one now and then settled, and stung and stung. Through the whole night, too, they pursued her in dreams with pitiless iteration and fantastic change; and at dawn she was awakened by voices calling up to her from the Ursulines' Garden,—the slim, pale nun crying out, in a lamentable accent, that all men were false and there was no shelter save the convent or the grave, and the comfortable sister bemoaning herself that on meagre days Madame de la Peltrie ate nothing but choke-cherries from Chateau-Bigot.

Kitty rose and dressed herself, and sat at the window, and watched the morning come into the garden below: first, a tremulous flush of the heavens; then a rosy light on the silvery roofs and gables; then little golden aisles among the lilacs and hollyhocks. The tiny flower-beds just under her window were left, with their snap-dragons and larkspurs, in dew and shadow; the small dog stood on the threshold, and barked uneasily when the bell rang in the Ursulines' Chapel, where the nuns were at matins.

It was Sunday, and a soft tranquillity blest the cool air in which the young girl bathed her troubled spirit. A faint anticipative homesickness mingled now with her nightlong anxiety,—a pity for herself that on the morrow she must leave those pretty sights, which had become so dear to her that she could not but feel herself native among them. She must go back to Eriecreek, which was not a walled city, and had not a stone building, much less a cathedral or convent, within its borders; and though she dearly loved those under her uncle's roof there, yet she had to own that, beyond that shelter, there was little in Eriecreek to touch the heart or take the fancy; that the village was ugly, and the village people mortally dull, narrow, and uncongenial. Why was not her lot cast somewhere else? Why should she not see more of the world that she had found so fair, and which all her aspirations had fitted her to enjoy? Quebec had been to her a rapture of beautiful antiquity; but Europe, but London, Venice, Rome, those infinitely older and more storied cities of which she had lately talked so much with Mr. Arbuton,—why should she not see them?

Here, for the guilty space of a heat-lightning flash, Kitty wickedly entertained the thought of marrying Mr. Arbuton for the sake of a bridal trip to Europe, and bade love and the fitness of things and the incompatibility of Boston and Eriecreek traditions take care of themselves. But then she blushed for her meanness, and tried to atone for it as she could by meditating the praise of Mr. Arbuton. She felt remorse for having, as he had proved yesterday, undervalued and misunderstood him; and she was willing now to think him even more magnanimous than his generous words and conduct showed him. It would be a base return for his patience to accept him from a worldly ambition; a man of his noble spirit merited the best that love could give. But she respected him; at last she respected him fully and entirely, and she could tell him that at any rate.

The words in which he had yesterday protested his love for her repeated themselves constantly in her revery. If he should speak them again after he had seen her in Boston, in the light by which she was anxious to be tested,—she did not know what she should say.

XIII

ORDEAL

They had not planned to go anywhere that day; but after
church they found themselves with the loveliest afternoon of
their stay at Quebec to be passed somehow, and it was a pity to
pass it indoors, the colonel said at their early dinner. They
canvassed the attractions of the different drives out of town,
and they decided upon that to Lorette. The Ellisons had
already been there, but Mr. Arbuton had not, and it was from
a dim motive of politeness towards him that Mrs. Ellison chose
the excursion; though this did not prevent her from wondering
aloud afterward, from time to time, why she had chosen it. He
was restless and absent, and answered at random when points
of the debate were referred to him, but he eagerly assented to
the conclusion, and was in haste to set out.

The road to Lorette is through St. John's Gate, down into the
outlying meadows and rye-fields, where, crossing and recro-
ssing the swift St. Charles, it finally rises at Lorette above the
level of the citadel. It is a lonelier road than that to Montmorenci, and the scattering cottages upon it have not the well-to-
do prettiness, the operatic repair, of stone-built Beauport. But
they are charming, nevertheless, and the people seem to be
remoter from modern influences. Peasant-girls, in purple
gowns and broad straw hats, and not the fashions of the year
before last, now and then appeared to our acquaintance; near
one ancient cottage an old man, in the true habitant's red
woollen cap with a long fall, leaned over the bars of his gate

and smoked a short pipe.

By and by they came to Jeune-Lorette, an almost ideally pretty hamlet, bordering the road on either hand with galleried and balconied little houses, from which the people bowed to them as they passed, and piously enclosing in its midst the village church and churchyard. They soon after reached Lorette itself, which they might easily have known for an Indian town by its unkempt air, and the irregular attitudes in which the shabby cabins lounged along the lanes that wandered through it, even if the Ellisons had not known it already, or if they had not been welcomed by a pomp of Indian boys and girls of all shades of darkness. The girls had bead-wrought moccasins and work-bags to sell, and the boys bore bows and arrows and burst into loud cries of "Shoot! shoot! grand shoot! Put-up-pennies! shoot-the-pennies! Grand shoot!" When they recognized the colonel, as they did after the party had dismounted in front of the church, they renewed these cries with greater vehemence.

"Now, Richard," implored his wife, "you're *not* going to let those little pests go through all that shooting performance again?"

"I must. It is expected of me whenever I come to Lorette; and I would never be the man to neglect an ancient observance of this kind." The colonel stuck a copper into the hard sand as he spoke, and a small storm of arrows hurtled around it. Presently it flew into the air, and a fair-faced, blue-eyed boy picked it up: he won most of the succeeding coins.

"There's an aborigine of pure blood," remarked the colonel; "his ancestors came from Normandy two hundred years ago. That's the reason he uses the bow so much better than these coffee-colored impostors."

They went into the chapel, which stands on the site of the ancient church burnt not long ago. It is small, and it is bare and rude inside, with only the commonest ornamentation about the altar, on one side of which was the painted wooden statue of a nun, on the other that of a priest,—slight enough commemoration of those who had suffered so much for the hopeless race that lingers and wastes at Lorette in incurable squalor and wildness. They are Christians after their fashion, this poor remnant of the mighty Huron nation converted by the Jesuits and crushed by the Iroquois in the far-western wilderness; but whatever they are at heart, they are still savage in countenance, and these boys had faces of wolves and foxes. They followed their visitors into the church, where there was only an old woman praying to a picture, beneath which hung a votive hand and foot, and a few young Huron suppliants with very sleek hair, whose wandering devotions seemed directed now at the strangers, and now at the wooden effigy of the House of St. Ann borne by two gilt angels above the high-altar. There was no service, and the visitors soon quitted the chapel amid the clamors of the boys outside. Some young girls, in the dress of our period, were promenading up and down the road with their arms about each other and their eyes alert for the effect upon spectators.

From one of the village lanes came swaggering towards the visitors a figure of aggressive fashion,—a very buckish young fellow, with a heavy black mustache and black eyes, who wore a jaunty round hat, blue checked trousers, a white vest, and a morning-coat of blue diagonals, buttoned across his breast; in his hand he swung a light cane.

"That is the son of the chief, Paul Picot," whispered the driver.

"Excuse me," said the colonel, instantly; and the young gentleman nodded. "Can you tell me if we could see the chief to-day?"

"O yes!" answered the notary in English, "my father is chief. You can see him"; and passed on with a somewhat supercilious air.

The colonel, in his first hours at Quebec, had bought at a

bazaar of Indian wares the photograph of an Indian warrior in a splendor of factitious savage panoply. It was called "The Last of the Hurons," and the colonel now avenged himself for the curtness of M. Picot by styling him "The Next to the Last of the Hurons."

"Well," said Fanny, who had a wife's willingness to see her husband occasionally snubbed, "I don't know why you asked him. I'm sure nobody wants to see that old chief and his wretched bead trumpery again."

"My dear," answered the colonel, "wherever Americans go, they like to be presented at court. Mr. Arbuton, here, I've no doubt has been introduced to the crowned heads of the Old World, and longs to pay his respects to the sovereign of Lorette. Besides, I always call upon the reigning prince when I come to Lorette. The coldness of the heir-apparent shall not repel me."

The colonel led the way up the principal lane of the village. Some of the cabins were ineffectually whitewashed, but none of them were so uncleanly within as the outside prophesied. At the doors and windows sat women and young girls working moccasins; here and there stood a well-fed mother of a family with an infant Huron in her arms. They all showed the traces of white blood, as did the little ones who trooped after the strangers and demanded charity as clamorously as so many Italians; only a few faces were of a clear dark, as if stained by walnut-juice, and it was plain that the Hurons were fading, if not dying out. They responded with a queer mixture of French liveliness and savage stolidity to the colonel's jocose advances. Great lean dogs lounged about the thresholds; they and the women and children were alone visible; there were no men. None of the houses were fenced, save the chief's; this stood behind a neat grass plot, across which, at the moment our travellers came up, two youngish women were trailing in long morning-gowns and eye-glasses. The chief's house was a handsome cottage, papered and carpeted, with a huge stove in the parlor, where also stood a table exposing the bead trumpery

W. D. Howells

of Mrs. Ellison's scorn. A full-bodied elderly man with quick, black eyes and a tranquil, dark face stood near it; he wore a half-military coat with brass buttons, and was the chief Picot. At sight of the colonel he smiled slightly and gave his hand in welcome. Then he sold such of his wares as the colonel wanted, rather discouraging than inviting purchase. He talked, upon some urgency, of his people, who, he said, numbered three hundred, and were a few of them farmers, but were mostly hunters, and, in the service of the officers of the garrison, spent the winter in the chase. He spoke fair English, but reluctantly, and he seemed glad to have his guests go, who were indeed willing enough to leave him.

Mr. Arbuton especially was willing, for he had been longing to find himself alone with Kitty, of which he saw no hope while the idling about the village lasted.

The colonel bought an insane watch-pocket for *une dolleur* from a pretty little girl as they returned through the village; but he forbade the boys any more archery at his expense, with "Pas de grand shoot, *now*, mes enfans!—Friends," he added to his own party, "we have the Falls of Lorette and the better part of the afternoon still before us; how shall we employ them?"

Mrs. Ellison and Kitty did not know, and Mr. Arbuton did not know, as they sauntered down past the chapel, to the stone mill that feeds its industry from the beauty of the fall. The cascade, with two or three successive leaps above the road, plunges headlong down a steep crescent-shaped slope, and hides its foamy whiteness in the dark-foliaged ravine below. It is a wonder of graceful motion, of iridescent lights and delicious shadows; a shape of loveliness that seems instinct with a conscious life. Its beauty, like that of all natural marvels on our continent, is on a generous scale; and now the spectators, after viewing it from the mill, passed for a different prospect of it to the other shore, and there the colonel and Fanny wandered a little farther down the glen, leaving Kitty with Mr. Arbuton. The affair between them was in such a puzzling phase, that there was as much reason for as against this: nobody could do anything, not even openly recognize it. Besides, it was somehow very interesting to Kitty to be there alone with him, and she thought that if all were well, and he and she were really engaged, the sense of recent betrothal could be nowhere else half so sweet as in that wild and lovely place. She began to imagine a bliss so divine, that it would have been strange if she had not begun to desire it, and it was with a half reluctant, half-acquiescent thrill that she suffered him to touch upon what was first in both their minds.

"I thought you had agreed not to talk of that again for the present," she feebly protested.

"No; I was not forbidden to tell you I loved you: I only consented to wait for my answer; but now I shall break my promise. I cannot wait. I think the conditions you make dishonor me," said Mr. Arbuton, with an impetuosity that fascinated her.

"O, how can you say such a thing as that?" she asked, liking him for his resentment of conditions that he found humiliating, while her heart leaped remorseful to her lips for having imposed them. "You know very well why I wanted to delay; and you know that—that—if—I had done anything to wound you, I never could forgive myself."

"But you doubted me, all the same," he rejoined.

"Did I? I thought it was myself that I doubted." She was stricken with sudden misgiving as to what had seemed so well; her words tended rapidly she could not tell whither.

"But why do you doubt yourself?"

"I—I don't know."

"No," he said bitterly, "for it's really me that you doubt. I can't understand what you have seen in me that makes you believe anything could change me towards you," he added with a kind of humbleness that touched her. "I could have borne to think that I was not worthy of you."

"Not worthy of me! I never dreamed of such a thing."

"But to have you suspect me of such meanness—"

"O Mr. Arbuton!"

—"As you hinted yesterday, is a disgrace that I ought not to bear. I have thought of it all night; and I must have my answer now, whatever it is."

She did not speak; for every word that she had uttered had only served to close escape behind her. She did not know what to do; she looked up at him for help. He said with an accent of meekness pathetic from him, "Why must you still doubt me?"

"I don't," she scarcely more than breathed.

"Then you are mine, now, without waiting, and forever," he cried; and caught her to him in a swift embrace.

She only said, "Oh!" in a tone of gentle reproach, yet clung to him a helpless moment as for rescue from himself. She looked at him in blank pallor, striving to realize the tender violence in which his pulses wildly exulted; then a burning flush dyed her face, and tears came into her eyes. "O, I hope you'll never be sorry," she said; and then, "Do let us go," for she had no distinct desire save for movement, for escape from that place.

Her heart had been surprised, she hardly knew how; but at his kiss a novel tenderness had leaped to life in it. She suffered him to put her hand upon his arm, and then she began to feel a strange pride in his being tall and handsome, and hers. But she kept thinking as they walked, "I hope he'll never he sorry," and she said it again, half in jest. He pressed her hand against his heart, and met her look with one of protest and reassurance, that presently melted into something sweeter yet. He said,

"What beautiful eyes you have! I noticed the long lashes when I saw you on the Saguenay boat, and I couldn't get away from them."

"O please, don't speak of that dreadful time!" cried Kitty.

"No? Why not?"

"O because! I think it was such a bold kind of accident my taking your arm by mistake; and the whole next day has always been a perfect horror to me."

He looked at her in questioning amaze.

"I think I was very pert with you all day,—and I don't think I'm pert naturally,—taking you up about the landscape, and twitting you about the Saguenay scenery and legends, you know. But I thought you were trying to put me down,—you are rather down-putting at times,—and I admired you, and I couldn't bear it."

"Oh!" said Mr. Arbuton. He dimly recollected, as if it had been in some former state of existence, that there were things he had not approved in Kitty that day, but now he met her penitence with a smile and another pressure of the hand. "Well, then," he said, "if you don't like to recall that time, let's go back of it to the day I met you on Goat Island Bridge at Niagara."

"O, did you see *me* there? I thought you didn't; but *I* saw *you*. You had on a blue cravat," she answered; and he returned with as much the air of coherency as if really continuing the same train of thought, "You won't think it necessary to visit Boston, now, I suppose," and he smiled triumphantly upon her. "I fancy that I have now a better right to introduce you there than your South End friends."

Kitty smiled, too. "I'm willing to wait. But don't you think you ought to see Eriecreek before you promise too solemnly? I can't allow that there's anything serious, till you've seen me at home."

They had been going, for no reason that they knew, back to the country inn near which you purchase admittance to a certain view of the falls, and now they sat down on the piazza, somewhat apart from other people who were there, as Mr. Arbuton said, "O, I shall visit Eriecreek soon enough. But I shall not come to put myself or you to the proof. I don't ask to see you at home before claiming you forever."

Kitty murmured, "Ah! you are more generous than I was."

"I doubt it."

"O yes, you are. But I wonder if you'll be able to find Eriecreek."

"Is it on the map?"

"It's on the county map; and so is Uncle Jack's lot on it, and a picture of his house, for that matter. They'll all be standing on the piazza—something like this one—when you come up. You'll know Uncle Jack by his big gray beard, and his bushy eyebrows, and his boots, which he won't have blacked, and his Leghorn hat, which we can't get him to change. The girls will be there with him,—Virginia all red and heated with having got supper for you, and Rachel with the family mending in her hand,—and they'll both come running down the walk to welcome you. How will you like it?"

Mr. Arbuton suspected the gross caricature of this picture, and smiled securely at it. "I shall like it well enough," he said, "if you run down with them. Where shall you be?"

"I forgot. I shall be up stairs in my room, peeping through the window-blinds, to see how you take it. Then I shall come down, and receive you with dignity in the parlor, but after supper you'll have to excuse me while I help with the dishes.

Uncle Jack will talk to you. He'll talk to you about Boston. He's much fonder of Boston than you are, even." And here Kitty broke off with a laugh, thinking what a very different Boston her Uncle Jack's was from Mr. Arbuton's, and maliciously diverted with what she conceived of their mutual bewilderment in trying to get some common stand-point. He had risen from his chair, and was now standing a few paces from her, looking toward the fall, as if by looking he might delay the coming of the colonel and Fanny.

She checked her merriment a moment to take note of two ladies who were coming up the path towards the porch where she was sitting. Mr. Arbuton did not see them. The ladies mounted the steps, and turned slowly and languidly to survey the company. But at sight of Mr. Arbuton, one of them advanced directly toward him, with exclamations of surprise and pleasure, and he with a stupefied face and a mechanical movement turned to meet her.

She was a lady of more than middle age, dressed with certain personal audacities of color and shape, rather than overdressed, and she thrust forward, in expression of her amazement, a very small hand, wonderfully well gloved; her manner was full of the anxiety of a woman who had fought hard for a high place in society, and yet suggested a latent hatred of people who, in yielding to her, had made success bitter and humiliating.

Her companion was a young and very handsome girl, exquisitely dressed, and just so far within the fashion as to show her already a mistress of style. But it was not the vivid New York stylishness. A peculiar restraint of line, an effect of lady-like concession to the ruling mode, a temperance of ornament, marked the whole array, and stamped it with the unmistakable character of Boston. Her clear tints of lip and cheek and eye were incomparable; her blond hair gave weight to the poise of her delicate head by its rich and decent masses. She had a look of independent innocence, an angelic expression of extremely nice young fellow blending with a subtle maidenly charm. She indicated her surprise at seeing

W. D. Howells

Mr. Arbuton by pressing the point of her sun-umbrella somewhat nervously upon the floor, and blushing a very little. Then she gave him her hand with friendly frankness, and smiled dazzlingly upon him, while the elder hailed him with effusive assertion of familiar acquaintance, heaping him with greetings and flatteries and cries of pleasure.

"O dear!" sighed Kitty, "these are old friends of his; and will I have to know them? Perhaps it's best to begin at once, though," she thought.

But he made no movement toward her where she sat. The ladies began to walk up and down, and he with them. As they passed her, he did not seem to see her.

The ladies said they were waiting for their carriage, which they had left at a certain point when they went to look at the fall, and had ordered to take them up at the inn. They talked about people and things that Kitty had never heard of.

"Have you seen the Trailings since you left Newport?" asked the elder woman.

"No," said Mr. Arbuton.

"Perhaps you'll be surprised then—or perhaps you won't—to hear that we parted with them on the top of Mount Washington, Thursday. And the Mayflowers are at the Glen House. The mountains are horribly full. But what are you to do! Now the Continent"—she spoke as if the English Channel divided it from us—"is so common, you can't run over there any more."

Whenever they walked towards Kitty, this woman, whose quick eye had detected Mr. Arbuton at her side as she came up to the inn, bent upon the young girl's face a stare of insolent curiosity, yet with a front of such impassive coldness that to another she might not have seemed aware of her presence. Kitty shuddered at the thought of being made acquainted with her; then she remembered, "Why, how stupid I am! Of course a gentleman can't introduce ladies; and the only thing for him to do is to excuse himself to them as soon as he can without rudeness, and come back to me." But none the less she felt helpless and deserted. Though ordinarily so brave, she was so beaten down by that look, that for a glance of not unkindly interest that the young lady gave her she was abjectly grateful. She admired her, and fancied that she could easily be friends with such a girl as that, if they met fairly. She wondered that she should be there with that other, not knowing that society cannot really make distinctions between fine and coarse, and could not have given her a reason for their association.

Still the three walked up and down before Kitty, and still she made his peace with herself, thinking, "He is embarrassed; he can't come to me at once; but he will, of course."

The elder of his companions talked on in her loud voice of this thing and that, of her summer, and of the people she had met, and of their places and yachts and horses, and all the splendors of their keeping,—talk which Kitty's aching sense sometimes caught by fragments, and sometimes in full. The lady used a slang of deprecation and apology for having come to such a queer resort as Quebec, and raised her brows when Mr. Arbuton reluctantly owned how long he had been there.

"Ah, ah!" she said briskly, bringing the group to a stand-still while she spoke, "one doesn't stay in a slow Canadian city a whole month for love of the *place*. Come, Mr. Arbuton, is she English or French?"

Kitty's heart beat thickly, and she whispered to herself, "O, now!—now surely he *must* do something."

"Or perhaps," continued his tormentor, "she's some fair fellow-wanderer in these Canadian wilds,—some pretty companion of voyage."

Mr. Arbuton gave a kind of start at this, like one thrilled for an

W. D. Howells

instant with a sublime impulse. He cast a quick, stealthy look at Kitty, and then as suddenly withdrew his glance. What had happened to her who was usually dressed so prettily? Alas! true to her resolution, Kitty had again refused Fanny's dresses that morning, and had faithfully put on her own travelling-suit,— the suit which Rachel had made her, and which had seemed so very well at Eriecreek that they had called Uncle Jack in to admire it when it was tried on. Now she knew that it looked countrified, and its unstylishness struck in upon her, and made her feel countrified in soul. "Yes," she owned, as she met Mr. Arbuton's glance, "I'm nothing but an awkward milkmaid beside that young lady." This was unjust to herself; but truly it was never in her present figure that he had intended to show her to his world, which he had been sincere enough in contemning for her sake while away from it. Confronted with good society in these ladies, its delegates, he doubtless felt, as never before, the vastness of his self-sacrifice, the difficulty of his enterprise, and it would not have been so strange if just then she should have appeared to him through the hard cold vision of the best people instead of that which love had illumined. She saw whatever purpose toward herself was in his eyes, flicker and die out as they fell from hers. Then she sat alone while they three walked up and down, up and down, and the skirts of the ladies brushed her garments in passing.

"O, where can Dick and Fanny be?" she silently bemoaned herself, "and why don't they come and save me from these dreadful people?"

She sat in a stony quiet while they talked on, she thought, forever. Their voices sounded in her ears like voices heard in a dream, their laughter had a nightmare cruelty. Yet she was resolved to be just to Mr. Arbuton, she was determined not meanly to condemn him; she confessed to herself, with a glimmer of her wonted humor, that her dress must be an ordeal of peculiar anguish to him, and she half blamed herself for her conscientiousness in wearing it. If she had conceived of any such chance as this, she would perhaps, she thought, have worn Fanny's grenadine.

She glanced again at the group which was now receding from her. "Ah!" the elder of the ladies said, again halting the others midway of the piazza's length, "there's the carriage at last! But what is that stupid animal stopping for? O, I suppose he didn't understand, and expects to take us up at the bridge! Provoking! But it's no use; we may as well go to him at once; it's plain he isn't coming to us. Mr. Arbuton, will you see us on board?"

"Who—I? Yes, certainly," he answered absently, and for the second time he cast a furtive look at Kitty, who had half started to her feet in expectation of his coming to her before he went,—a look of appeal, or deprecation, or reassurance, as she chose to interpret it, but after all a look only.

She sank back in blank rejection of his look, and so remained motionless as he led the way from the porch with a quick and anxious step. Since those people came he had not openly recognized her presence, and now he had left her without a word. She could not believe what she could not but divine, and she was powerless to stir as the three moved down the road towards the carriage. Then she felt the tears spring to her eyes: she flung down her veil, and, swept on by a storm of grief and pride and pain, she hurried, ran towards the grounds about the falls. She thrust aside the boy who took money at the gate. "I have no money," she said fiercely; "I'm going to look for my friends: they're in here."

But Dick and Fanny were not to be seen. Instead, as she fluttered wildly about in search of them, she beheld Mr. Arbuton, who had missed her on his return to the inn, coming with a frightened face to look for her. She had hoped, somehow never to see him again in the world; but since it was to be, she stood still and waited his approach in a strange composure; while he drew nearer, thinking how yesterday he had silenced her prophetic doubt of him: "I have one answer to all this; I love you." Her faltering words, verified so fatally soon, recalled themselves to him with intolerable accusation. And what should he say now? If possibly,—if by some miracle,—she might not have seen what he feared she must!

W. D. Howells

One glance that he dared give her taught him better; and while she waited for him to speak, he could not lure any of the phrases, of which the air seemed full, to serve him.

"I wonder you came back to me," she said after an eternal moment.

"Came back?" he echoed, vacantly.

"You seemed to have forgotten my existence!"

Of course the whole wrong, if any wrong had been done to her, was tacit, and much might be said to prove that she felt needlessly aggrieved, and that he could not have acted otherwise than as he did; she herself had owned that it must be an embarrassing position to him.

"Why, what have I done," he began, "what makes you think... For heaven's sake listen to me!" he cried; and then, while she turned a mute attentive face to him, he stood silent as before, like one who has lost his thought, and strives to recall what he was going to say. "What sense,—what use," he resumed at last, as if continuing the course of some previous argument, "would there have been in making a display of our acquaintance before them? I did not suppose at first that they saw us together."... But here he broke off, and, indeed, his explanation had but a mean effect when put into words. "I did not expect them to stay. I thought they would go away every moment; and then at last it was too late to manage the affair without seeming to force it." This was better; and he paused again, for some sign of acquiescence from Kitty, and caught her eye fixed on his face in what seemed contemptuous wonder. His own eyes fell, and ran uneasily over her dress before he lifted them and began once more, as if freshly inspired: "I could have wished you to be known to my friends with every advantage on your side," and this had such a magnanimous sound that he took courage; "and you ought to have had faith enough in me to believe that I never could have meant you a slight. If you had known more of the world,—if your social experience had been greater you would have seen.... Oh!" he cried, desperately, "is there nothing you have to say to me?"

"No," said Kitty, simply, but with a languid quiet, and shrinking from speech as from an added pang. "You have been telling me that you were ashamed of me in this dress before those people. But I knew that already. What do you want me to do?"

"If you give me time, I can make everything clear to you."

"But now you don't deny it."

"Deny what? I—"

But here the whole fabric of Mr. Arbuton's defence toppled to the ground. He was a man of scrupulous truth, not accustomed to deceive himself or others. He had been ashamed of her, he could not deny it, not to keep the love that was now dearer to him than life. He saw it with paralyzing clearness; and, as an inexorable fact that confounded quite as much as it dismayed him, he perceived that throughout that ignoble scene she had been the gentle person and he the vulgar one. How could it have happened with a man like him! As he looked back upon it, he seemed to have been only the helpless sport of a sinister chance.

But now he must act; it could not go so, it was too horrible a thing to let stand confessed. A hundred protests thronged to his lips, but he refused utterance to them all as worse even than silence; and so, still meaning to speak, he could not speak. He could only stand and wait while it wrung his heart to see her trembling, grieving lips.

His own aspect was so lamentable, that she half pitied him, half respected him for his truth's sake. "You were right; I think it won't be necessary for me to go to Boston," she said with a dim smile. "Good by. It's all been a dreadful, dreadful mistake."

It was like him, even in that humiliation, not to have thought of losing her, not to have dreamed but that he could somehow repair his error, and she would yet willingly be his. "O no, no, no," he cried, starting forward, "don't say that! It can't be, it mustn't be! You are angry now, but I know you'll see it differently. Don't be so quick with me, with yourself. I will do anything, say anything, you like."

The tears stood in her eyes; but they were cruel drops. "You can't say anything that wouldn't make it worse. You can't undo what's been done, and that's only a little part of what couldn't be undone. The best way is for us to part; it's the only way."

"No, there are all the ways in the world besides! Wait—think!—I implore you not to be so—precipitate."

The unfortunate word incensed her the more; it intimated that she was ignorantly throwing too much away. "I am not rash now, but I was very rash half an hour ago. I shall not change my mind again. O," she cried, giving way, "it isn't what you've done, but what you *are* and what *I* am, that's the great trouble! I could easily forgive what's happened,—if you asked it; but I couldn't alter both our whole lives, or make myself over again, and you couldn't change yourself. Perhaps you would try, and I know that I would, but it would be a wretched failure and disappointment as long as we lived. I've learnt a great deal since I first saw those people." And in truth he felt as if the young girl whom he had been meaning to lift to a higher level than her own at his side had somehow suddenly grown beyond him; and his heart sank. "It's foolish to try to argue such a thing, but it's true; and you must let me go."

"I *can't* let you go," he said in such a way, that she longed at least to part kindly with him.

"You can make it hard for me," she answered, "but the end will be the same."

"I won't make it hard for you, then," he returned, after a pause, in which he grew paler and she stood with a wan face plucking the red leaves from a low bough that stretched itself towards her.

He turned and walked away some steps; then he came suddenly back. "I wish to express my regret," he began formally, and with his old air of doing what was required of him as a gentleman, "that I should have unintentionally done anything to wound—"

"O, better not speak of *that*," interrupted Kitty with bitterness, "it's all over now." And the final tinge of superiority in his manner made her give him a little stab of dismissal. "Good by. I see my cousins coming."

She stood and watched him walk away, the sunlight playing on his figure through the mantling leaves, till he passed out of the grove.

The cataract roared with a seven-fold tumult in her ears, and danced before her eyes. All things swam together, as in her blurred sight her cousins came wavering towards her.

"Where is Mr. Arbuton?" asked Mrs. Ellison.

Kitty threw her arms about the neck of that foolish woman, whoso loving heart she could not doubt, and clung sobbing to her. "Gone," she said; and Mrs. Ellison, wise for once, asked no more.

She had the whole story that evening, without asking; and whilst she raged, she approved of Kitty, and covered her with praises and condolences.

"Why, of course, Fanny, I didn't care for *knowing* those people. What should I want to know them for? But what hurt me was that he should so postpone me to them, and ignore me before them, and leave me without a word, then, when I ought to have been everything in the world to him and first of all. I believe things came to me while I sat there, as they do to drowning people, all at once, and I saw the whole affair more distinctly than ever I did. We were too far apart in what we had been and what we believed in and respected, ever to grow really together. And if he gave me the highest position in the world, I should have only that. He never could like the people who had been good to me, and whom I loved so dearly, and he only could like me as far as he could estrange me from them. If he could coolly put me aside *now*, how would it be afterwards with the rest, and with me too? That's what flashed through me, and I don't believe that getting splendidly married is as good as being true to the love that came long before, and honestly living your own life out, without fear or trembling, whatever it is. So perhaps," said Kitty, with a fresh burst of tears, "you needn't condole with me so much, Fanny. Perhaps if you had seen him, you would have thought he was the one to be pitied. *I* pitied him, though he *was* so cruel. When he first turned to meet them, you'd have thought he was a man sentenced to death, or under some dreadful spell or other; and while he was walking up and down listening to that horrible comical old woman,—the young lady didn't talk much,—and trying to make straight answers to her, and to look as if I didn't exist, it was the most ridiculous thing in the world."

"How queer you are, Kitty!"

"Yes; but you needn't think I didn't feel it. I seemed to be like two persons sitting there, one in agony, and one just coolly watching it. But O," she broke out again while Fanny held her closer in her arms, "how could he have done it, how could he have acted so towards me; and just after I had begun to think him so generous and noble! It seems too dreadful to be true." And with this Kitty kissed her cousin and they had a little cry together over the trust so done to death; and Kitty dried her eyes, and bade Fanny a brave good-night, and went off to weep again, upon her pillow.

But before that, she called Fanny to her door, and with a smile breaking through the trouble of her face, she asked, "How do you suppose he got back? I never thought of it before."

"*Oh!*" cried Mrs. Ellison with profound disgust, "I hope he had to *walk* back. But I'm afraid there were only too many chances for him to ride. I dare say he could get a calash at the hotel there."

Kitty had not spoken a word of reproach to Fanny for her part in promoting this hapless affair; and when the latter, returning to her own room, found the colonel there, she told him the story and then began to discern that she was not without credit for Kitty's fortunate escape, as she called it.

"Yes," said the colonel, "under exactly similar circumstances she'll know just what to expect another time, if that's any comfort."

"It's a *great* comfort," retorted Mrs. Ellison; "you can't find out what the world is, too soon, I can tell you; and if I hadn't maneuvered a little to bring them together, Kitty might have gone off with some lingering fancy for him; and think what a misfortune that would have been!"

"Horrible."

"And now, she'll not have a single regret for him."

"I should think not," said the colonel; and he spoke in a tone of such dejection, that it went to his wife's heart more than any reproach of Kitty's could have done. "You're all right, and nobody blames you, Fanny; but if *you* think it's well for such a girl as Kitty to find out that a man who has had the best that the world can give, and has really some fine qualities of his own, can be such a poor devil, after all, then *I* don't. She may be the wiser for it, but you know she won't be the happier."

"O *don't*, Dick, don't speak seriously! It's so dreadful from *you*. If you feel so about it, why don't you do something."

"O yes, there's a fine opening. We know, because we know ever so much more, how the case really is; but the way it seems to stand is, that Kitty couldn't bear to have him show civility to his friends, and ran away, and then wouldn't give him a chance to explain. Besides, what could I do under any circumstances?"

"Well, Dick, of course you're right, and I wish I could see things as clearly as you do. But I really believe Kitty's glad to be out of it."

"What?" thundered the colonel.

"I think Kitty's secretly relieved to have it all over. But you needn't *stun* me."

"You *do*?" The colonel paused as if to gain force enough for a reply. But after waiting, nothing whatever came to him, and he wound up his watch.

"To be sure," added Mrs. Ellison thoughtfully, after a pause, "she's giving up a great deal; and she'll probably never have such another chance as long as she lives."

"I hope she won't," said the colonel.

"O, you needn't pretend that a high position and the social advantages he could have given her are to be despised."

"No, you heartless worldling; and neither are peace of mind, and self-respect, and whole feelings, and your little joke."

"O, you—you sickly sentimentalist!"

"That's what they used to call us in the good old abolition days," laughed the colonel; and the two being quite alone, they made their peace with a kiss, and were as happy for the moment as if they had thereby assuaged Kitty's grief and mortification.

"Besides, Fanny," continued the colonel, "though I'm not much on religion, I believe these things are ordered."

"Don't be blasphemous, Colonel Ellison!" cried his wife, who represented the church if not religion in her family. "As if Providence had anything to do with love-affairs!"

"Well, I won't; but I will say that if Kitty turned her back on Mr. Arbuton and the social advantages he could offer her, it's a sign she wasn't fit for them. And, poor thing, if she doesn't know how much she's lost, why she has the less to grieve over. If she thinks she couldn't be happy with a husband who would keep her snubbed and frightened after he lifted her from her lowly sphere, and would tremble whenever she met any of his own sort, of course it may be a sad mistake, but it can't be helped. She must go back to Eriecreek, and try to worry along without him. Perhaps she'll work out her destiny some other way."

XIV

AFTERWARDS

Mrs. Ellison had Kitty's whole story, and so has the reader, but for a little thing that happened next day, and which is perhaps scarcely worthy of being set down.

Mr. Arbuton's valise was sent for at night from the Hotel St. Louis, and they did not see him again. When Kitty woke next morning, a fine cold rain was falling upon the drooping hollyhocks in the Ursulines' Garden, which seemed stricken through every leaf and flower with sudden autumn. All the forenoon the garden-paths remained empty, but under the porch by the poplars sat the slender nun and the stout nun side by side, and held each other's hands. They did not move, they did not appear to speak.

The fine cold rain was still falling as Kitty and Fanny drove down Mountain Street toward the Railway Station, whither Dick and the baggage had preceded them, for they were going away from Quebec. Midway, their carriage was stopped by a mass of ascending vehicles, and their driver drew rein till the press was over. At the same time Kitty saw advancing up the sidewalk a figure grotesquely resembling Mr. Arbuton. It was he, but shorter, and smaller, and meaner. Then it was not he, but only a light overcoat like his covering a very common little man about whom it hung loosely,—a burlesque of Mr. Arbuton's self-respectful overcoat, or the garment itself in a state of miserable yet comical collapse.

"What is that ridiculous little wretch staring at you for, Kitty?" asked Fanny.

"I don't know," answered Kitty, absently.

The man was now smiling and gesturing violently. Kitty remembered having seen him before, and then recognized the cooper who had released Mr. Arbuton from the dog in the Sault au Matelot, and to whom he had given his lacerated overcoat.

The little creature awkwardly unbuttoned the garment, and took from the breast-pocket a few letters, which he handed to Kitty, talking eagerly in French all the time.

"What *is* he doing, Kitty?"

"What is he saying, Fanny?"

"Something about a ferocious dog that was going to spring upon you, and the young gentleman being brave as a lion and rushing forward, and saving your life." Mrs. Ellison was not a woman to let her translation lack color, even though the original wanted it.

"Make him tell it again."

When the man had done so, "Yes," sighed Kitty, "it all happened that day of the Montgomery expedition; but I never knew, before, of what he had done for me. Fanny," she cried, with a great sob, "may be I'm the one who has been cruel? But what happened yesterday makes his having saved my life seem such a very little matter."

"Nothing at all!" answered Fanny, "less than nothing!" But her heart failed her.

The little cooper had bowed himself away, and was climbing the hill, Mr. Arbuton's coat-skirts striking his heels as he walked.

"What letters are those?" asked Fanny.

"O, old letters to Mr. Arbuton, which he found in the pocket. I suppose he thought I would give them to him."

"But how are you going to do it?"

"I ought to send them to him," answered Kitty. Then, after a silence that lasted till they reached the boat, she handed the letters to Fanny. "Dick may send them," she said.

ABOUT THE AUTHOR

William Dean Howells (March 1, 1837 – May 11, 1920) was an American realist author and literary critic.

Born in Martins Ferry, Ohio, originally Martinsville, to William Cooper and Mary Dean Howells, Howells was the second of eight children. His father was a newspaper editor and printer, and the father moved frequently around Ohio. Howells began to help his father with typesetting and printing work at an early age. In 1852, his father arranged to have one of Howells' poems published in the Ohio State Journal without telling him.

He wrote his first novel, The Wedding Journey, in 1872, but his literary reputation took off with the realist novel, A Modern Instance, published in 1882, which described the decay of a marriage. His 1885 novel The Rise of Silas Lapham is perhaps his best known, describing the rise and fall of an American entrepreneur in the paint business. His social views were also strongly reflected in the novels Annie Kilburn (1888) and A Hazard of New Fortunes (1890). He was particularly outraged by the trials resulting from the Haymarket Riot.

In 1904, he was one of the first seven chosen for membership in the American Academy of Arts and Letters, of which he became president.

Choose from Thousands of 1stWorldLibrary Classics By

A. M. Barnard
Ada Leverson
Adolphus William Ward
Aesop
Agatha Christie
Alexander Aaronsohn
Alexander Kielland
Alexandre Dumas
Alfred Gatty
Alfred Ollivant
Alice Duer Miller
Alice Turner Curtis
Alice Dunbar
Allen Chapman
Alleyne Ireland
Ambrose Bierce
Amelia E. Barr
Amory H. Bradford
Andrew Lang
Andrew McFarland Davis
Andy Adams
Angela Brazil
Anna Alice Chapin
Anna Sewell
Annie Besant
Annie Hamilton Donnell
Annie Payson Call
Annie Roe Carr
Annonaymous
Anton Chekhov
Archibald Lee Fletcher
Arnold Bennett
Arthur C. Benson
Arthur Conan Doyle
Arthur M. Winfield
Arthur Ransome
Arthur Schnitzler
Arthur Train
Atticus
B.H. Baden-Powell
B. M. Bower
B. C. Chatterjee
Baroness Emmuska Orczy
Baroness Orczy
Basil King
Bayard Taylor
Ben Macomber
Bertha Muzzy Bower
Bjornstjerne Bjornson

Booth Tarkington
Boyd Cable
Bram Stoker
C. Collodi
C. E. Orr
C. M. Ingleby
Carolyn Wells
Catherine Parr Traill
Charles A. Eastman
Charles Amory Beach
Charles Dickens
Charles Dudley Warner
Charles Farrar Browne
Charles Ives
Charles Kingsley
Charles Klein
Charles Hanson Towne
Charles Lathrop Pack
Charles Romyn Dake
Charles Whibley
Charles Willing Beale
Charlotte M. Braeme
Charlotte M. Yonge
Charlotte Perkins Stetson
Clair W. Hayes
Clarence Day Jr.
Clarence E. Mulford
Clemence Housman
Confucius
Coningsby Dawson
Cornelis DeWitt Wilcox
Cyril Burleigh
D. H. Lawrence
Daniel Defoe
David Garnett
Dinah Craik
Don Carlos Janes
Donald Keyhoe
Dorothy Kilner
Dougan Clark
Douglas Fairbanks
E. Nesbit
E. P. Roe
E. Phillips Oppenheim
E. S. Brooks
Earl Barnes
Edgar Rice Burroughs
Edith Van Dyne
Edith Wharton

Edward Everett Hale
Edward J. O'Biren
Edward S. Ellis
Edwin L. Arnold
Eleanor Atkins
Eleanor Hallowell Abbott
Eliot Gregory
Elizabeth Gaskell
Elizabeth McCracken
Elizabeth Von Arnim
Ellem Key
Emerson Hough
Emilie F. Carlen
Emily Bronte
Emily Dickinson
Enid Bagnold
Enilor Macartney Lane
Erasmus W. Jones
Ernie Howard Pie
Ethel May Dell
Ethel Turner
Ethel Watts Mumford
Eugene Sue
Eugenie Foa
Eugene Wood
Eustace Hale Ball
Evelyn Everett-green
Everard Cotes
F. H. Cheley
F. J. Cross
F. Marion Crawford
Fannie E. Newberry
Federick Austin Ogg
Ferdinand Ossendowski
Fergus Hume
Florence A. Kilpatrick
Fremont B. Deering
Francis Bacon
Francis Darwin
Frances Hodgson Burnett
Frances Parkinson Keyes
Frank Gee Patchin
Frank Harris
Frank Jewett Mather
Frank L. Packard
Frank V. Webster
Frederic Stewart Isham
Frederick Trevor Hill
Frederick Winslow Taylor

Friedrich Kerst
Friedrich Nietzsche
Fyodor Dostoyevsky
G.A. Henty
G.K. Chesterton
Gabrielle E. Jackson
Garrett P. Serviss
Gaston Leroux
George A. Warren
George Ade
Geroge Bernard Shaw
George Cary Eggleston
George Durston
George Ebers
George Eliot
George Gissing
George MacDonald
George Meredith
George Orwell
George Sylvester Viereck
George Tucker
George W. Cable
George Wharton James
Gertrude Atherton
Gordon Casserly
Grace E. King
Grace Gallatin
Grace Greenwood
Grant Allen
Guillermo A. Sherwell
Gulielma Zollinger
Gustav Flaubert
H. A. Cody
H. B. Irving
H.C. Bailey
H. G. Wells
H. H. Munro
H. Irving Hancock
H. R. Naylor
H. Rider Haggard
H. W. C. Davis
Haldeman Julius
Hall Caine
Hamilton Wright Mabie
Hans Christian Andersen
Harold Avery
Harold McGrath
Harriet Beecher Stowe
Harry Castlemon
Harry Coghill
Harry Houidini

Hayden Carruth
Helent Hunt Jackson
Helen Nicolay
Hendrik Conscience
Hendy David Thoreau
Henri Barbusse
Henrik Ibsen
Henry Adams
Henry Ford
Henry Frost
Henry James
Henry Jones Ford
Henry Seton Merriman
Henry W Longfellow
Herbert A. Giles
Herbert Carter
Herbert N. Casson
Herman Hesse
Hildegard G. Frey
Homer
Honore De Balzac
Horace B. Day
Horace Walpole
Horatio Alger Jr.
Howard Pyle
Howard R. Garis
Hugh Lofting
Hugh Walpole
Humphry Ward
Ian Maclaren
Inez Haynes Gillmore
Irving Bacheller
Isabel Cecilia Williams
Isabel Hornibrook
Israel Abrahams
Ivan Turgenev
J.G.Austin
J. Henri Fabre
J. M. Barrie
J. M. Walsh
J. Macdonald Oxley
J. R. Miller
J. S. Fletcher
J. S. Knowles
J. Storer Clouston
J. W. Duffield
Jack London
Jacob Abbott
James Allen
James Andrews
James Baldwin

James Branch Cabell
James DeMille
James Joyce
James Lane Allen
James Lane Allen
James Oliver Curwood
James Oppenheim
James Otis
James R. Driscoll
Jane Abbott
Jane Austen
Jane L. Stewart
Janet Aldridge
Jens Peter Jacobsen
Jerome K. Jerome
Jessie Graham Flower
John Buchan
John Burroughs
John Cournos
John F. Kennedy
John Gay
John Glasworthy
John Habberton
John Joy Bell
John Kendrick Bangs
John Milton
John Philip Sousa
John Taintor Foote
Jonas Lauritz Idemil Lie
Jonathan Swift
Joseph A. Altsheler
Joseph Carey
Joseph Conrad
Joseph E. Badger Jr
Joseph Hergesheimer
Joseph Jacobs
Jules Vernes
Julian Hawthrone
Julie A Lippmann
Justin Huntly McCarthy
Kakuzo Okakura
Karle Wilson Baker
Kate Chopin
Kenneth Grahame
Kenneth McGaffey
Kate Langley Bosher
Kate Langley Bosher
Katherine Cecil Thurston
Katherine Stokes
L. A. Abbot
L. T. Meade

L. Frank Baum
Latta Griswold
Laura Dent Crane
Laura Lee Hope
Laurence Housman
Lawrence Beasley
Leo Tolstoy
Leonid Andreyev
Lewis Carroll
Lewis Sperry Chafer
Lilian Bell
Lloyd Osbourne
Louis Hughes
Louis Joseph Vance
Louis Tracy
Louisa May Alcott
Lucy Fitch Perkins
Lucy Maud Montgomery
Luther Benson
Lydia Miller Middleton
Lyndon Orr
M. Corvus
M. H. Adams
Margaret E. Sangster
Margret Howth
Margaret Vandercook
Margaret W. Hungerford
Margret Penrose
Maria Edgeworth
Maria Thompson Daviess
Mariano Azuela
Marion Polk Angellotti
Mark Overton
Mark Twain
Mary Austin
Mary Catherine Crowley
Mary Cole
Mary Hastings Bradley
Mary Roberts Rinehart
Mary Rowlandson
M. Wollstonecraft Shelley
Maud Lindsay
Max Beerbohm
Myra Kelly
Nathaniel Hawthrone
Nicolo Machiavelli
O. F. Walton
Oscar Wilde

Owen Johnson
P.G. Wodehouse
Paul and Mabel Thorne
Paul G. Tomlinson
Paul Severing
Percy Brebner
Percy Keese Fitzhugh
Peter B. Kyne
Plato
Quincy Allen
R. Derby Holmes
R. L. Stevenson
R. S. Ball
Rabindranath Tagore
Rahul Alvares
Ralph Bonehill
Ralph Henry Barbour
Ralph Victor
Ralph Waldo Emmerson
Rene Descartes
Ray Cummings
Rex Beach
Rex E. Beach
Richard Harding Davis
Richard Jefferies
Richard Le Gallienne
Robert Barr
Robert Frost
Robert Gordon Anderson
Robert L. Drake
Robert Lansing
Robert Lynd
Robert Michael Ballantyne
Robert W. Chambers
Rosa Nouchette Carey
Rudyard Kipling
Saint Augustine
Samuel B. Allison
Samuel Hopkins Adams
Sarah Bernhardt
Sarah C. Hallowell
Selma Lagerlof
Sherwood Anderson
Sigmund Freud
Standish O'Grady
Stanley Weyman
Stella Benson
Stella M. Francis

Stephen Crane
Stewart Edward White
Stijn Streuvels
Swami Abhedananda
Swami Parmananda
T. S. Ackland
T. S. Arthur
The Princess Der Ling
Thomas A. Janvier
Thomas A Kempis
Thomas Anderton
Thomas Bailey Aldrich
Thomas Bulfinch
Thomas De Quincey
Thomas Dixon
Thomas H. Huxley
Thomas Hardy
Thomas More
Thornton W. Burgess
U. S. Grant
Upton Sinclair
Valentine Williams
Various Authors
Vaughan Kester
Victor Appleton
Victor G. Durham
Victoria Cross
Virginia Woolf
Wadsworth Camp
Walter Camp
Walter Scott
Washington Irving
Wilbur Lawton
Wilkie Collins
Willa Cather
Willard F. Baker
William Dean Howells
William le Queux
W. Makepeace Thackeray
William W. Walter
William Shakespeare
Winston Churchill
Yei Theodora Ozaki
Yogi Ramacharaka
Young E. Allison
Zane Grey

www.ingramcontent.com/pod-product-compliance
Lightning Source LLC
Chambersburg PA
CBHW031345170626
46807CB00002B/843

* 9 7 8 1 4 2 1 8 4 0 1 6 1 *